Lady Action™

AIRSHIP 27 PRODUCTIONS

Lady Action: The Sands of Forever

Published by Airship 27 Productions
www.airship27.com
www.airship27hangar.com

Editor: Ron Fortier
Associate Editors: Fred Adams Jr., Gordon Dymowski
Marketing and Promotions Manager: Michael Vance
Production and design by Rob Davis.

ISBN-13: 978-0692459454 (Airship 27)
ISBN-10: 0692459456

Printed in the United States of America

10 9 8 7 6 5 4 3 2 1

Lady Action™

THE SANDS OF FOREVER

BY RON FORTIER

This one is for my pal from across the bay, Ian Watson. A better research resource no pulp writer ever had.
—Ron Fortier

A.C.T.I.O.N.
(*A*dvanced *C*ommand for *T*elluric *I*nterdiction *O*bservation and *N*ullifcation.)

A secret, international organization operating independent of world governments and dedicated to defending the earth from alien menaces and super-criminals of all types.

❋❋❋

Alan Porter drove his dented old Land Rover over the hardscrabble terrain of the Libyan Desert. His wheels raced over the stony, barren plain of one of the driest, most uninhabitable locales on the planet. The brutal afternoon sun beat down on the tan colored Rover as it made its way into the empty landscape; one of the harshest parts of the bigger Sahara Desert.

He passed very few oases as he continued to watch the ball-compass he'd tacked to his dashboard to assure he didn't veer astray from the route drawn over the yellowed map he'd procured from a Bedouin friend. Reaching the Great Sand Sea, he slowed the Rover and finally shut off the engine.

Climbing out of the auto, he withdrew his steel canteen and took a small drink. It was never wise to be greedy in a place where water was so vital to survival. He capped the canteen, dropped it back into his Rover and then retrieved a pair of German binoculars.

He pushed his sunglasses atop his thinning black hair and peered into the eye-slots.

Miles and miles of desert glass spread out before him and he wondered for the hundredth time if he wasn't on some kind of fool's errand. Still, as an agent of A.C.T.I.O.N., it was his primary mission to investigate the unknown and bizarre. Which was certainly the case in this solo excursion into such a foreboding place.

The landmark he was looking for should have been within a mile, if he hadn't gone too far off. His old compass was one he'd had for years and it had never failed him before. Then he spotted a long, curving shadow up ahead to the left and realized he was in fact looking at the crest of a giant dune.

He readjusted his sunglasses, got back in the Land Rover and started the engine again. Five minutes later he had rolled up the embankment and was looking down into a hidden vale beneath the dune's peak. Seeing no safe way to navigate his Rover down the steep slope, Porter, jumped out of the Rover, and began walking down the dune, doing his best to keep his balance as his booted feet dug into the hot, soft sand.

The further he went down the more impressive the area became to him. It was as if he was looking into a pool of liquid shadows, totally impenetrable to his eyes. It was simply an inky blackness. Then he was stumbling onto the level plateau and turning about to face the weird plot lost in the dune's protective shadow.

There was something there, something tall and straight. Porter reached into his khaki shorts and brought out his cell-phone. He walked closer towards the darkened area and as he did, the object at its center became clear.

It was a tree! A massive wooden affair with huge limbs covered by thousands of leaves that reached a good thirty feet high.

But that was impossible! How on earth could a leaf-bearing arbor like this exist in such a desolate place? As his feet crossed the shadow barrier, Porter raised his cell-phone and began snapping pictures. The tiny flash from his phone lit up the miracle tree in tiny blinking fashion and the closer he approached the more in awe he became. Then the leaves began to rustle and cooling wind was born from nowhere. He heard a humming noise and it seem to come from all around him, growing louder with each passing second.

Porter's right hand dropped to the butt of the .45 automatic holstered on his right hip.

Fear crept into him and he sensed for the first time he was not alone in this unnatural, hidden alcove with the impossible tree.

Then from behind the tree, coming out of the very walls of the mighty dune, he saw moving shadows that became human-like. The humming music reached a crescendo as the moving things suddenly came at him and for the first time he saw the knives in their hands. But by then it was too late and Porter knew he was dead.

With one final thought of defiance, he punched the send icon on his phone just as the ominous shadows enveloped his body.

***

The brightly colored birds erupted from the jungle canopy and took to the misty heavens with echoing flaps of their massive wings. It was enough to startle Jikem Khatel, who had been half asleep in the wooden guard shack outside the iron gates of the Eternal Light Compound.

Nestled back into the side of Kauai island's Mount Wai'ale'ale, the four acre estate was hidden from view by both the ten foot stone wall that surrounded three of its sides and the ever present rain fog. Located three fourths of the way to the mountain's 5,148 feet summit, hidden structures that made up the compound were all but invisible in one of the most isolated locales in the world: smack dab in the middle of the beautiful Hawaiian Islands.

Jikem, a former African mercenary with years of experience fighting in more wars than he could remember, peeled off his black beret and stuck his head out the open window to watch the gaggle of exotic birds as they flew off in multiple directions. Something had startled them. His right hand dropped to the handle of his automatic pistol holstered on his right hip. He scratched the back of his head, sweat from the thick humidity trickling down his big unshaven jaw.

At first he assumed some animal had come along through the brush to spook the birds as often happened. There was only the one tiny road that connected the estate with the world below and it was miles away from the public hiking trails of which there were only a few. Being one of the wettest locations on the planet, the ground was usually a saturated nightmare of gooey gray mud and there was no actual access to the summit other than by helicopter.

Thus the huge, burly guard was very surprised when the young woman came walking out of the heavy wet mist holding a hiking staff in her right hand and carrying a light-weight canvas backpack. Jikem actually blinked several times, set his beret squarely on his head and then rubbed his eyes to ascertain he wasn't daydreaming. But he was not and as he lowered his hands, the woman was even closer. She was of average height (maybe 5'7" or 8") he guessed, with a very trim, fit body wearing tough-leather hiking boots with thick white socks. She had on tan shorts that showed off her bronze thighs and legs with an old army belt circling her waist. Affixed to this were several pouches and a pair of leather gloves. She had on a light-weight, short-sleeve poplin shirt over a dark blue sports bra, a checkered kerchief tied about her neck and Rayban sunglasses. The hand wielding the five foot staff was decorated with an expensive mountaineer's watch which not only told time but was a working compass.

The brutish Jikem took all this in within seconds, having learned over the years how to quickly assess strangers who might in the end prove to be a threat. The fact that he had survived so long only testified to just how good he was at this. Still, the one item of clothing on the unexpected hiker that caught his attention was her hat. Normally, when down in the village gathering supplies, he saw many tourists such as this one and they either sported a floppy camouflage hat or some chic baseball cap. But not this trim, good looking female with jet black hair that was cut short.

She wore a yachting cap cocked at a rakish angle.

And she was whistling what sounded like "Rule Britannia".

Jikem hit the call button on the intercom unit before him while keeping his eyes on the approaching woman.

"DeSale here," came the crackling voice of his boss, Henri DeSale, from the main house. "What is it?"

"A girl hiker, she just came out of the jungles to the south-east."

There was a pause and then Jikem heard a whirring of gears overhead. DeSale had swiveled the camera set atop the stone wall near the gate to get a better view of the stranger.

"I see her. Okay, find out what she wants and get rid of her."

"Yes, sir." He stepped out of the guard shack and stood with his back to the seven foot tall iron gate, his arms folded across his chest. At 6 feet, four inches tall, Jikem Khatel was an impressive figure, his powerful body exuding physical strength.

The female hiker, having been seen, was now approaching him directly, her steps hastening slightly.

"Thank God," she blurted out with a distinctive British accent. "I thought I'd never find my way off this bloody mountain."

"This is private property," Jikem informed her, his face a mask of non-interest. "You can't go beyond this point."

"Okay, big fellow. Don't get your knickers in a bunch. I just got lost, love. I'm here on vacation and thought I'd check out the local fauna and all."

"The public hiking trails are on the other side of the mountain. You need to go."

"All right, mate. Just give me a second, if you please?" She suddenly shoved her staff at him and Jikem instinctively reached out and took hold of it. The woman pointed to the small dirt road, while flipping off her backpack with a shrug. "That's the main road back down to the village, I take it."

"Yes, it is the only way to and from here."

"I see." From the canvas pack she pulled out a canteen, uncapped it and took a long swallow. Then she wiped her mouth with the back of her hand and put it away. "Well, then I guess I better get on with it."

She reached out her hand for the staff and Jikem handed it back to her. She clamped her hand over his and suddenly twisted the long pole so as to trap his right thumb. It folded back and pain shot through his arm.

"Aggh."

Her left boot came up between his legs and smashed into his crotch. Jikem's eyes doubled and before he could give out with another cry, she spun around fast and slammed the hardwood staff into his right temple with a loud crack. She stepped aside smoothly as the burly sentry toppled onto his face into the mud unconscious.

***

Tossing her staff to the ground next to her backpack, Nicola Sinclair, Agent of A.C.T.I.O.N., took hold of the guard's feet and with a mighty effort dragged him to the front of the small guard shack.

"*What the bloody hell are you doing?*" The voice from her sophisticated earbud suddenly demanded.

"What's it look like?" she replied while entering the guard post and searching the control panel for the switch that would open the gates. "I'm proceeding to locate and rescue the objective."

"*That was not your primary directive,*" the annoyed male voice reminded her. "*Your primary directive was to learn the objective's whereabouts and then, if feasible, call in a strike team to assist you in retrieving said objective.*"

Sinclair found the proper button and hit it. With a rusty groan, the two halves of the gate began to open outward. At the same time a clanging alarm sounded from the main building. She was well aware her taking out the guard had been witnessed on the closed circuit TV camera and she would soon have company; the angry sort.

"Look, Byron, love, I simply got tired of sitting around." She reached outside, grabbed her backpack off the ground and set it on the small table, next to the stack of girlie magazines and empty beer cans. From it she pulled out a .45 Caliber British Ranger automatic and several additional clips which she stuffed into the pockets of her cargo-shorts.

"*Damn it girl, we don't even know how many men they've got.*"

"Which is why I'm counting on you and my magic hat," Sinclair said as she took hold of the hard bill of her cap and activated its amazing technological properties by pressing it between her fingers. Instantly an array of microchip sensors and diodes began collecting data and transmitting it back to Byron Walters, her Mission Controller back at A.C.T.I.O.N. headquarters in London via satellite.

"Oh, I'm sure the Brotherhood of Oppressed People's Army has no shortage of employees. As I recall, the Polynesian police report of the kidnapping indicated at least a half dozen men were involved."

"Then you won't be surprised when I tell you that at least that many just emerged from the compound's center structure and are now approaching you rapidly."

Sinclair then dug into her supplies one more time and found three smoke whiz-bang grenades.

"Okay, Byron love, time to go to work."

She dashed out of the guard hut and through the open gates. The ever present mountain fog made it difficult to see what was ahead of her clearly, but that was also easily remedied with a tap to the corner of her special sunglasses. Having infrared lens capabilities, what were at first only vague shapes moving towards her morphed into blazing red human shapes which she could clearly identify. She yanked out the pin from one of the whiz-bangs and threw it out towards the main house and the oncoming terrorists. Then she dropped to one knee, aimed and fired away. She hit three of the guards before the round noisy smoke grenade exploded. Whiz-bangs gave off a screeching sound at the same time their chemical core poured thick smoke into the air.

Having caused havoc and confusion, Sinclair rose to her feet and charged onward through the thick smoky barrier. Her head swiveled back and forth, watching for heat figures. One popped up to her right and she blasted him into oblivion. Men were screaming and crying all around her; most were wounded while others were blinded and unable to find a target to shoot at.

"Six meters to the front entrance."

"Thank you, Byron dear."

The porch appeared magically before her and she leapt to it just as the door swung open. Sinclair fired a hole through the armed man about to emerge and his body rocketed back into the gloomy interior.

She rushed inside scoping out the wide area before her while she continued to feed her intel.

"You're in the main lounge. Picking up two bodies heading your way from

a back room, another two from a hallway to your right and three more coming down from the second floor to your immediate left. Time to move, girl!"

It took her seconds to mentally establish the furniture lay-out before her, the two over stuffed leather sofas, several matching chairs, a wet-bar near the door Byron had mentioned. The staircase was to her left and she could hear heavy footsteps and men shouting. Sinclair bolted across the living area and dove over the far sofa landing roughly on the hardwood floor behind it. Pressed between the sofa and wall, she stilled her breathing as her foes all converged on the room.

Steps trampled down the stairs while a door banged. All seven men had come together not ten feet away from her.

"It's a woman!" one of them said. "I saw her take out Jikem and open the gates then we lost her as she charged up to the house."

"Well, by the hole in Kanme's chest over there, I'd say she made it inside."

Sinclair recognized several different accents and knew her cap receiver was picking up their voices loud and clear. Sure enough, Byron was back with what she'd already suspected.

"Confirm, the one giving the orders is Henri DeSale, leader of this cell. Terminate with extreme prejudice."

Easy for you to say, Sinclair thought, keeping herself still in her narrow hidey hole. Sure, it would be a bonus to take out a world-class terrorist like DeSale, but that wasn't her mission. Somewhere in this place there was a frightened teenage girl who needed rescuing. If these nut-jobs hadn't already killed her.

"How could one girl do all this?" another of the terrorists spoke up.

She could hear the confusion in his voice. Good.

"She's probably the advance scout for a larger strike force," DeSale put forth. "Regardless, she and who knows how many others, are in the compound. We have to retaliate immediately or none of us will get off this island alive!"

There were several agreeing comments, then DeSale spoke again. "Fathar, you check on the girl in the cellar, while the rest of you spread out. Bollo, you and Milner check the grounds and see how many of our men are still fighting out there. Pedro, you and I will check the rest of the house!"

And with that, Sinclair heard the group dispersing in various directions. She popped her head up from behind the sofa in time to see one fellow rush off down a corridor by himself. That had to be the one called Fathar.

She ripped off her sunglasses, stuffed them into the top pocket of her shirt and then vaulted over the settee. In one smooth, gymnastic move, she landed on her feet in a crouch, then silently sprang up and went after the single kidnapper; all the while clutching her automatic and staying alert.

"Are they gone?" she whispered to her controller listening back in England.

"Affirmative. The chap you are following appears to moving towards a portal that descends into the building's basement. Be wary, the cement walls might blur our satellite imagery if you go down there. You'll be on your own."

"Really. And what was I up till now?"

"Why part of team, darling. As always."

"Funny, the only other players on this pitch seem to be members of the other side."

Up ahead Fathar had turned a corner. Sinclair increased her pace while hugging the wall and planting her feet as softly as she could. At the corner she stopped and peeked to see what came next. Not ten feet away, the big man had opened a door and was vanishing behind it. She moved fast.

Just as Byron had indicated, it was the entrance to the sublevel and as she came up to it she could see Fathar stomping down wooden steps into a stygian darkness below. Without hesitating, Sinclair started down the stairs rapidly purposely slapping her hiking boots on the steps to be heard by her prey.

With only five more steps to take before reaching the floor, Fathar, hearing her, turned around puzzled to see what was behind him. Thus, Sinclair jumped off her own step, twisting her body about in mid-air and threw out a snap kick with her right leg. It hit the Fathar in the face mashing his nose like candy brittle and knocking him backwards. He gave up a muffled cry, his arms pin-wheeling desperately to maintain his balance but it was impossible.

His body came off the step and he fell down the remaining distance so that his head crashed into the cement wall at the bottom of the stairs. There was a loud cracking noise as his neck broke and he died instantly, his body crumbling in a heap.

Whereas Sinclair, landed hard on her feet and almost lost her own balance but like a cat, reached out with her empty left hand and grabbed the stairs to hold herself up.

"Who's there?" a frightened voice asked from the blackness before her.

The A.C.T.I.O.N. agent spotted a light switch just above Fathar's fallen body and flicked it on. A single, naked light bulb hanging from the ceiling rafters lit up the square room. Stacked against the walls were crates and all manner of machinery giving evidence that the room was primarily used for storage.

But now it also did double duty as a prison. Seated directly under the dangling light, was a young teenaged black girl whose right leg was chained by a steel manacle that bolted into the floor. Dressed in a skimpy green bikini, the frightened captive's eyes were wide with fear, as she clutched herself in the room's humid dampness. She was almost bald, her hair cut severely short in a style currently popular among South African girls.

Sinclair recognized her from the pictures she had been provided. She was Antuay Mulama, the daughter of the South African Ambassador to Great Britain who had been snatched two days earlier while on vacation with several of her school mates in Polynesia.

"Who are you?" she asked as Sinclair approached her and knelt to examine the manacle about her right ankle.

"My name is Niki. I've been sent to rescue you." She put down her pistol and snapped opened a pouch on her belt.

Antuay looked from Sinclair to the dead terrorist and then the stairs. "How many of you are there?"

"Just me, darling," Sinclair smiled having retrieved a small plastic tube. "Now I need you to stretch out your foot and hold it steady."

"What? You're alone!"

Sinclair patted Antuay's scuffed knee. "Darling, we really don't have much time. I need you to trust me and do everything I tell you. If you do that, then I will get you out of here and home safe."

The poor girl looked into her eyes and then nodded.

"Good girl, now hold up that leg with the manacle."

Antuay did as she was told and Sinclair positioned the foot over her own right knee. Then taking the small tube, she uncapped it and very carefully poured a small amount of liquid into the manacle's locking pin-hole.

"What is that?"

There was a sizzling sound and then the manacle popped open.

"A special kind of acid that melts steel." Sinclair capped the tiny tube and tossed it aside. Then she reclaimed her pistol and extended her hand to the now freed prisoner.

"Come along, we really need to move fast!"

Together they started up the stairs, the frightened black girl staying right behind Sinclair, who moved upward with her gun arm extended. As she came out of the stairwell, two of DeSale's men appeared to her right charging down the hallway. Sinclair fired two quick rounds dropping them like ten-pins in a bowling alley.

"Come on!" she urged Antuay as she jogged down the corridor and without halting, leaped over the two dead men. The girl copied her movements and Sinclair led her back to the main area of the house. The last place their searchers would be looking for them to appear was the front door. So that's the route Sinclair chose, knowing fully well that if she guessed wrong they would be cut down the second they exited the place.

The front door was still open and she raced out over the porch and onto the front yard. Most of the thick smoke her whiz-bangs had produced had now been blown away from strong mountain gusts of wet air and the field before them to the front gate was completely visible.

"Ah, there you are, love. We've got you back on line."

The tiny voice in her ear startled her for a second. "I really don't have time for this now, Byron. Shut up for a second."

"But I didn't say anything," the confused girl said behind her.

"Not you, dear." Sinclair tapped her right ear with the barrel of her automatic. "The busy-bodies back home."

"I heard that."

Between them and the gate were another three men, all carrying light-weight Israeli Uzi submachine guns. Two of them were in the process of examining the men she had shot during her assault to see if any were still alive while the third was marching towards the guard-house, his weapon at ready should other invaders be lurking in the surrounding brush beyond the muddy road.

Without slowing her pace, Sinclair shot the two nearest guards and then pointed her gun at the man by the gate. He spun around and fired a quick burst. Clumps of dirt exploding on the ground in front of them and Antuay screamed, hiding herself behind the British agent.

Sinclair held the British Ranger steady, squeezed the trigger and fought the recoil as the jacketed slug flew straight and hit her target in the head. Blood and gore spewed from the back of his ruined skull as he fell over like a fallen timber.

"Keep moving, love. The others in the house are all converging on the front entrance and are going to be on your heels in a second."

"Understood," Sinclair replied as she and Antuay dashed through the open gate. She looked at the beautiful young girl and gave her an approving smile before pointing to the tree line of the jungle. "In there, stay right behind me!"

As she pushed through the dense green brush, Sinclair did her best to make the path less formidable for her young charge. The kidnapped girl was doing her best to keep up with her rescuer although still shaken by the nightmarish events of the past few days.

"Where are we?" Antuay asked pushing aside a massive frond.

"Hawaii," Sinclair told her, ducking under a tree limb. "Kauai to be exact."

"Really! I had no idea. When those men grabbed me on Bora Bora, they gave me some kind of drug that knocked me out. When I awoke, I was back there in that cellar. I had no way of knowing where I was."

They continued moving through the jungle at a good clip. Whereas Byron was blessedly silent, Sinclair assumed their pursuers had given up the chase for the time being. Or at least that was her hope; as slim as it might be.

"How did you find me?" The girl's curiosity was only natural.

"I work for an international police organization known as A.C.T.I.O.N. Within hours of your abduction, my people were able to track every single flight out of Bora Bora and learn their destinations. Of those, three had the best odds of being your kidnappers. When the other two landed, other agents were there to greet them. When they proved to be legitimate, I was ordered here to find you."

"You are amazing!"

"No applause yet, please. We are not out of the woods yet."

"What do you mean? I don't hear anyone chasing us."

"We can't make it down this mountain on foot. They know that and unless I'm wrong, we're about to see them again very soon."

"Then how can we get away?"

Niki Sinclair pushed through more brush and stepped into a mist shrouded clearing where she had parked her ride. "In this," she said, sweeping out her hand towards the strange vehicle before them. Antuay stopped beside her and tried to catch her breath as she looked upon the strange looking vehicle; if that's what it was?

The auto was small, long and sleek. It reminded the African girl of a giant metallic tadpole as its main part was a round cab covered by a clear plastic canopy that sat on one large rubber tire. Then its body extended from behind it like one long tail covered over by two long struts and ended at a short steel fin affixed over two smaller wheels. Antuay had seen fuel-efficient "smart" cars before, but this contraption, painted blue and red, was like something out of a science-fiction movie.

"Climb in!" Sinclair ordered as she easily flipped open the front bubble and pointed to the two black bucket seats inside. Seeing the steering wheel to the left, the girl picked up her leg and settled herself into the right seat. Sinclair tossed her pistol onto the console between the seats and then jumped in easily. She flicked a knob on the control board and the bubble cover dropped back over them. She snapped it shut and then pressed the start button to the right of the steering column and the weird automobile's engine roared to life. Antuay felt a slight vibration.

"Buckle up, dear," Sinclair said as she did likewise. Then she grabbed the wheel, stomped down on the gas pedal and the mechanical tadpole rolled forward. It plowed through the underbrush crushing twigs and branches until it emerged onto the muddy, narrow trail road. She steered it to the left and sent them speeding downward.

The oddly shaped vehicle was hard to control as its three wheels found little traction in the inches deep mud surface of the worn path. As they continued downward, Antuay noticed the pea-soup like cloud of mist was evaporating rapidly as strong winds from the valley below made themselves known. Then in the blink of an eye everything before them was revealed with stark clarity and the surprised girl screamed.

The sky before them was a sharp cerulean with wispy clouds that seemed painted over the white-capped waters of the ocean far away. But it wasn't this beautiful vista that had shaken Antuay Mulama but rather the steep road down which they were hurtling.

They were racing down a slope with the mountain's thick foliage to their left and immediately to their right was the cliff's edge which they skirted dangerously. There were no barriers whatsoever and a mistake on the driver's part would send them plunging over the drop-off and swiftly to a horrible death thousands of feet below.

Antuay had never been afraid of heights…until now. As Sinclair pulled on the wheel to bring them around a sharp curve, their bizarre auto came within mere inches of the rocky cliff and she had an unimpeded few of the verdant valley far, far beneath them.

"Heads up, Niki, darling, several of your terrorists chums have left the compound on what appear to be all terrain vehicles and are quickly gaining on your position!"

Sinclair turned her glance towards the rear-view mirror affixed to the center of the front windshield bubble just as she heard gunshots from behind. Sure enough, members of the outlaw gang were racing at them on four-wheeled carts. Through the dirt and mud they were kicking up, and the fact they had to travel the narrow road in single-file, she quickly counted three…maybe four pursuers. Each wore racing goggles and wielded an Uzi. It was the nearest who had fired a quick burst, although firing one-handed, his aim had been totally off the mark.

"Keep your head down," Sinclair ordered as she maintained her tight grip on the steering wheel and took them around yet another sharp corner. Their unique car's tail end whipped around behind them and its back fin passed over the cliff's edge as she fought to keep them on the road.

More gunshots sounded and several bullets hit the fuselage. Bad shooting or not, it was only inevitable that once the terrorists overtook them in their faster ATVs, they would have no problems riddling their vehicle to look like Swiss cheese.

"Okay," Sinclair said, touching her earbud. "Time for us to spread our wings and fly."

"Good luck, Sinclair. For your information, a detachment of United States Marines has been dispatched from the U.S.S. New York and is on route to your destination."

"Well, better late than never, old chap."

Bullets pinged off the canopy over their heads. Sinclair reached to a red-painted lever on the floor pad between the seats. Antuay watched as she gripped it firmly and pulled it back. Their auto shook as motors behind them began to whir loudly. The scared girl managed to raise her head slightly and look back over her shoulder.

The twin strut panels that ran the length of their vehicles were coming apart, each folding out away from the other like…wings!

"What's happening?" she queried her rescuer.

"It's time we said goodbye to these bad boys, wouldn't you say?"

"Goodbye?"

"Hold your breath …and close your eyes, Antuay."

Sinclair pulled the wheel into a hard right turn and the airomobile shot off the cliff and plummeted. Antuay would have screamed, but her stomach flipped and nothing came out of her mouth as they fell. G-forces pushed against them, shoving each of them into the pads of their seats, the safety belts holding them both in place. Then the girl felt the entire airomobile shudder as the wings reached their full extension, locked into place and caught the air.

Sinclair pulled back hard and the flying car shot upward from its dive and swooped away from the mountain leaving the startled terrorists far behind. Like a giant metal gull, the airomobile flew over the valley and she flew them into a south-westerly course towards the island's beaches of Pakala and Waimea in the distance.

Raising her head above the console, Antuay gasped. "We're flying!"

"Indeed, we are."

"Your car…it's a flying machine."

"The Airomobile .03 Cloud Climber to be specific," Sinclair smiled. "They tell me in another few years everyone will have one of these. It's really a Brave New World, isn't it?"

They were flying over the villages now and Antuay looked down to see dozens of hotels and tourist resorts. Ant-size people covered the golden sands enjoying the sun and surf. Her mind attempted to digest the fact that these people, enjoying an earthly paradise below, had no idea of the hell she had undergone only a few miles away from that mountain.

"Here come the Marines," Sinclair announced and pointed ahead.

The girl looked up to see two large, turtle green helicopters flying in their direction. They were headed straight for Mount Wai'ale'ale. As they passed, she could see heavily armed Marines inside and the pilot of the lead chopper gave them the thumbs-up signal.

"Go get 'em, Yanks," Sinclair returned the greeting.

"Where are we going?" Antuay saw they were continuing towards the watery horizon. Below there was nothing but deep blue sea.

"Up ahead, dear. You can't miss it."

Then, as if rising up out of the Pacific, there on the water was a massive aircraft carrier *U.S.S. New York.*

"You can relax now," Sinclair said banking to the right to line them up properly with the floating runway before them. "We'll have you home safe in a wink, now."

Antuay turned and looked at her savior. "Thank you…and I don't even know your name?"

"Well, that is rather confidential…but, you can call me Lady Action."

❋❋❋

Nicola Sinclair downshifted her gunmetal gray 2006 Chrysler Crossfire SE two-seater convertible roadster as she rolled through the center of Sleaford; a quaint market town and civil parish in the North Kesteven district of Lincolnshire. Located in the East Midlands of England, Sleaford sat on the edge of the fertile Fenlands and was surrounded by acres of cabbage fields.

It was early August and a distant, friendly sun gazed down from powder blue skies as she drove over the tiny culverted river that ran under the town's high street. She passed the spectacular St. Deny's Church on her right as she headed north towards the revitalized industrial section. Hatless, she wore her Rayban sunglasses and had a white silk scarf wrapped around her neck, its tail trailing in the wind as she drove along.

Sleaford was all she loved about her homeland, its country folk with their rich history and traditions, its small shops and boutiques, its isolated farms and rustic beauty. Ever aware of the pedestrians on the crowded sidewalks, she calmly tapped the brake pedal when a runaway soccer ball suddenly appeared out of nowhere and dropped onto the road in front of her. It was soon followed by a towheaded young boy in playing shorts who dashed out into the street to scoop it up and then gave her a friendly wave before vanishing again.

Sinclair smiled, shifted up a gear, and sent her fancy German-made sports car out of the town square and back onto a rural straightaway. She gently gave the V6 engine more petrol and gradually increased her speed. She loved the sleek Crossfire with its broad rear fenders and distinctive boat-tail rear end. With its wide wheelbase, the low-to-the-ground roadster hugged the road like a moving magnet and the exhilaration of racing through the countryside was euphoric.

As an active A.C.T.I.O.N. agent, Sinclair spent more time abroad than she did in her own native England and any opportunity she had to take the sexy Crossfire out of the garage and blow out its carburetors was too strong a temptation to resist. Thus the reason she never considered taking the train up from London where she kept a flat.

She passed a few farmers on the narrow road coming in from the fields in their old, beat up hauling trucks and she waved to them happily. An optimist from birth, Niki Sinclair loved these rare opportunities to be carefree and simply enjoy the simple things in life: a beautiful day, an open road and her speedy roadster. Sometimes life was very, very good.

Sinclair wasn't surprised when two low-flying Hawk T2 military jets swooped overhead with a loud roar and flew off in the opposite direction. Lincolnshire had been the home of the RAF Bomber Command during World War II and over two hundred working airfields dotted the county. The ready access to these airfields had been one of the factors in locating A.C.T.I.O.N. command in the area.

Eventually she spotted the A.C.T.I.O.N. complex with its long, modern two story building surrounded by smaller constructions. A giant plaque facing the road had bold letters indicating the company's bogus name, Avalon Creative Telemarketing & International Operations Networks. Her rear tires kicked up tiny gravel pieces as she drove into the huge parking section. As she sought out an empty spot, she calculated the lot held approximately a hundred cars. It never ceased to amuse her that one of the world's most sophisticated international peace keeping organizations was located in the middle of a British countryside, out in the open for all the world to see and take note of.

As she brought the Crossfire to an abrupt stop, she recalled the old saying, "The best place to hide something was in plain sight."

Climbing out of the right driver's side, Sinclair slung her large carry purse and began marching towards the main entrance. She wore a light tan overcoat belted at the waist and shiny black boots with flat heels. She walked past well kept lawns, a fountain to her right and a flower garden to her left. Several gardeners in coveralls were busy trimming hedges and adding mulch to several healthy ferns.

The genius behind A.C.T.I.O.N. headquarters lay in the fact that the building before her was in fact a real international marketing enterprise funded by A.C.T.I.O.N. that employed several hundred people from accountants to advertising managers all the way down to mail room clerks and secretaries. And according to what she was told, the company was actually very profitable, providing much of the funding for the clandestine parent outfit's many sophisticated gadgets like her tech-saturated yachting cap now nestled in her purse.

Entering the main lobby, Sinclair walked past the long reception counter and gave a friendly nod to the two young ladies working there. As she was a familiar face, they both said their hellos as she continued past them. They assumed she was on her way to one of the offices on the second floor.

She was not.

Sinclair passed the four elevators located around the corner from the lobby and continued around a second corner where she went directly to a janitor's closet. Taking a quick glance to make sure there was no one in the corridor to see her, she entered the closet, closed the door behind her and then turned to face the tiny enclosure's back wall.

The secret agent looked up at the single light fixture and said, "Code name, Lady Action." The light turned red and a scanning glow covered her entire face for a split second. Then the light was yellow again, indicating her retinal scan had been approved. Had it not recognized her, an alarm would have sounded in the security offices located in the underground facility she was about to enter.

Against the back wall was a shelf filled with various cleaning bottles, she reached out and pressed a hidden button. A soft whirring noise accompanied the false wall opening into a secret lift. Once inside, she tapped the single red button; the door closed and the elevator started down to the secret level beneath the basement. She turned to face the opposite wall and when the lift came to a gentle rest, it slid open to reveal the heart of Britain's A.C.T.I.O.N. command center.

The central room was circular and from it six corridors branched out like the spokes of a wheel. At the middle was the communication core with giant PC monitors displaying detailed maps of the entire globe; across these hundreds of tiny lights flashed. Each represented A.C.T.I.O.N. activities currently in progress. These desks were manned by specialists and controlled by several supervisors who were in constant motion from one radio-operation to the next.

Although there were a few people in regular civilian clothing, most at the stations were dressed in the standard A.C.T.I.O.N. uniform which consisted of black combat boots, a one piece blue jumper with red piping along the outer legs and sleeves, a black leather belt onto which was affixed a holster and automatic weapon. On the right shoulder of each tunic was a patch showing the A.C.T.I.O.N. logo of a globe superimposed over a naval anchor.

"Well, look who has deemed to grace us with her presence at long last," said Assistant Director Byron Fitzwalter as he appeared from one of the adjoining corridors. Dressed in Italian shoes, dress slacks, a cardigan sweater and an outlandish purple bow-tie, Fitzwalter was a short fellow, with a round, cherub like face, a small nose and two large blue eyes. His graying hair was stylishly cut and appeared to have been trimmed by a kitchen blender. He reminded Sinclair of a living marionette freed of its strings.

"Excuse me? I didn't know there was any urgency to my return."

An unabashed soul, Fitzwalter took hold of Sinclair's shoulders and gave her a kiss on the cheek. "You'd know if you'd kept your phone on," he chided upon releasing her. "The Commander is fit to be tied."

Sinclair took off her glasses, stuffed them into her purse and handed it to her friend who was also her primary field controller. "What's going on?"

"I'd best let her tell you. She's waiting for you in Conference Room Three along with Carl Durkins."

"From Data Analysis?"

"The one and the same, sweetie. Now get along."

"All right, all right." She pointed to her large purse. "My duty cap is in there. Be a dear and take it down to the gadget boys and have them tune it up for me."

"All right." He waved her toward one of the hallway branches. "Now shoo before we're both in hot water. You know the woman has no patience."

"Indeed, I do. Thanks, Byron."

The two parted company and Nicola Sinclair increased her pace as she made her way down the long corridor. Dozens of A.C.T.I.O.N. personnel greeted her as she walked along. A few minutes later she reached a door marked C-3. Taking a breath, she took hold of the knob and pulled the door open and entered.

***

"Agent Sinclair, how nice of you to join us." The sarcasm dripped like poisoned honey from the Commander's lips.

Sinclair closed the door behind her and looked directly at her boss standing at the end of a long rectangular conference table. It was a state of the art computer enhanced station with a clear quartz top and eight personal keypads. Of the eight padded chairs, only one was occupied by a middle-aged man wearing a tweed jacket, bifocals and smoking a pipe. The aromatic smell of cherrywood wafted through the enclosed room and out circulating vents.

She recognized Carl Durkins, the organization's financial wizard.

At the furthest end from the single door the Commander stood, arms folded severely across her chest. Her statuesque beauty, even in her fifties, always awed Sinclair. From what she knew personally, the woman, who stood six feet tall, with a dancer's lithe body, had been one of the leading super-models of her day. Of course that had been an MI-6 cover and a brilliant one. Who would ever suspect a woman whose face appeared on hundreds of fashion magazine covers around the world of being one of England's top spies. It had been an illustrious career until a botched assassination attempt with a faulty car-bomb had left her crippled; her left leg had been amputated at the knee.

"I'm sorry to have kept you waiting," Sinclair said hoping to avoid any further harsh words. "The weather has been so beautiful, I decided to drive up instead of taking the train."

"We know," the Commander's face never cracked.

Of course. What the hell don't you know?

As ever the Commander wore a dark gray pants suit, with a white silk blouse and a single gold necklace about her graceful neck. *She's so damn beautiful still,* Sinclair thought and hoped it had to do with good genes. Those high cheekbones, dark penetrating green eyes under arched brows and that wave of chestnut brown hair that refused to go gray; though a few strands were visible if one knew where to look.

I'll bet she's wearing heels. Initially the model/spy had thought her career finished because of her handicap. She had resigned herself to retirement and becoming a more hands-on mother to her only child then in secondary school. Then a representative of A.C.T.I.O.N. appeared at her door one day wanting to recruit her to run their new British headquarters that was still under construction at the time. At first she'd thought the fellow mad as well as blind. She'd pointed to her missing foot and asked, "What about that?"

The answer she received was beyond anything she could ever had imagined, or hoped for. Two days later she was driven to a hidden research laboratory in Manchester and there was shown a new prosthetic leg that appeared to be an exact replica of her missing limb in every detail, from the shape of her toes to the color of her tanned skin. The A.C.T.I.O.N. scientists went on to explain how her new leg would act and feel like a real flesh and blood leg…only it would better. It would be stronger, impervious to any kind of damage and within its core were several powerful micro-turbines that packed the punch of an ornery mule.

Of course she hadn't believed any of their silly claims. Still, to placate them, she had reluctantly agreed to try it on. The second she stood, her old sense of balance had returned instantly. Tentatively she'd begun walking about the lab with the nervous fear it was all a dream and she would ultimately collapse into a pitiful heap before these strange miracle workers. But she didn't fall once and by the end of the day she had donned sweats and running shoes and jogged two miles around the building. Her final act, before officially accepting the role of Britain's A.C.T.I.O.N. Commander was to kick down a steel door weighing eight hundred pounds with her new left leg.

Once again she was back in the game and motherhood took a back seat.

Everyone who worked at Sleaford knew the story inside and out. The

Commander was someone they all respected and even feared at times. Even Sinclair, who had even greater reasons to do so.

Moving towards the chair opposite the smoking Durkin, Sinclair untied her overcoat and peeled it off to drape it over one of the empty chairs.

"Hello, Mr. Durkin, good to see you again."

"Likwise, Agent Sinclair."

When the Commander saw her attire, Sinclair dropped her head slightly to hide her mischievous smile.

During a mission to the U.S. years earlier, Nicola Sinclair had worked with Miles Drake, the agent known throughout the intelligence community as Captain Action. Upon her return to England, she had fashioned a uniform to mimic his. It consisted of her black riding boots and leather mini-skirt under which she wore grey tights. She wore a sky-blue pull-over jersey with black sleeves and over the bosom had stitched the red-green-yellow triangle that encircled the embroidered white letters CA. About her slim waist was a black utility belt and matching holster in which rested her Eagle Ranger automatic. She wore it on her left hip although she was ambidextrous and a crack-shot using either hand.

Sinclair was well aware her boss didn't approve of the outfit but as an active field agent, it was her decision alone as how to dress. That it irked the Commander was an added bonus.

"Good work on the rescue of Miss Mulama. Her father was most generous in his comments to the Prime Minister."

"Thank you. I'm glad I was able to get to her in time. We put a nice crimp in the Brotherhoods's future plans."

"Yes, but unfortunately their leader was able to elude the marines and managed to escape the island."

Sinclair had started to pull out a chair and stopped. "DeSale is still free?"

"Yes," the Commander unfolded her arms and reached down to tap the table in front of her. "We've a world-wide search in progress, but that is not our primary concern at the moment, Agent Sinclair."

Sinclair sat and turned her chair to better face the Commander who was tapping the monitor before her. Instantly the entire wall became a high-definition video screen on which a man's photograph appeared. Sinclair recognized him immediately.

"You are familiar with Agent Alan Porter."

"Yes, Sir. We've worked together on several missions. He's one of our best people."

The Commander tapped another key and Porter's image shrunk to take up only the left half of the wall while the right now had a map of Libya and its neighboring countries.

"A week ago, while on assignment in Libya, Agent Porter failed to make his routine contact check-in. Per our standard operating procedures, his controller noted the absence and the Sensitive Issue Clock was started. When forty-eight hours had elapsed without any further contact, a ground team from Egypt was deployed. They were unable to discover his whereabouts and he is now officially listed as Status Unknown."

Sinclair felt her stomach tighten. That particular designation was not one likely declared and it generally meant the agent in question had been terminated by parties unknown.

"So what was Porter doing in Libya?" she asked, her attention totally focused on the Commander's briefing.

Now the wall images faded to be replaced by a video scene of a gala soiree with rich expensive limousines arriving in front of a cinema theater and thousands of celebrity seekers cheering from beyond cordoned areas. The paparazzi were in full force snapping away as international film stars emerged from the limos. One particular blonde in a dazzling white gown appeared and Sinclair recognized her as a well known American singer/actress. Accompanying the ingénue was a suave looking fellow in a dark dinner jacket. The camera moved in closer and the picture froze on a Mediterranean looking face with sharp features like a hawk and a trimmed brown mustache and goatee that matched his neatly cut hair. What Sinclair noticed immediately was a thin white scar running down the man's left cheek from his eyebrow.

"Arman El Shaira, a playboy millionaire of Algerian descent. He inherited most of his wealth from his father, the Sheik of Bakar who made all his money in oil. When the old man was assassinated eight years ago, his estate went to Arman and his younger sister, Falal. Although Falal runs the family empire, Arman is its public face and he works at acting the bon vivant jetsetter such as in his appearance at this year's Cannes Film Festival."

The Commander turned her back on the giant picture and tapped a few more keys. Now they were watching a scene in a different kind of movie, one obviously taken by some kind of spyware. They were looking through an open window at a meeting being held with men in Arab garb.

"This was shot five months ago in Cairo. The men seated in that room are all known Muslim terrorists." No sooner had the Commander's words left her mouth then Arman El Shaira was seen entering the room followed by two big men in western suits. He immediately embraced those people awaiting him. "We weren't able to get any sound bugs in the room but our tech people with lip-reading skills were able to glean some phrases. Enough to cause us concern.

"El Shaira at one point tells the others what they have all been searching for has been found. At which point there is heightened excitement and lots more hugging. Words like 'the holy' and 'by the will of Allah' are bandied about several times before the meeting ends and they depart."

"That sounds ominous enough when coming from terrorists like these," Sinclair offered. "I take it this has to do with Porter's going missing in Libya."

The Commander shut off the wall display and nodded. "Yes, it does. I brought in Agent Porter because of his experiences in that part of the world. His mission was simple enough, shadow El Shaira and learn what he and his associates were up to.

"The trail led to Libya; specifically the port of Tripoli." The Commander turned to Director Durkin. "Carl, why don't you continue from this point."

"Of course," the financial expert removed the pipe from his mouth and turned to Sinclair. "As you know, over the years most intelligence agencies have come to rely on the simple expedience of locating various outlaw regimes by investigating their financial holdings. Following the money trail, if you will.

"Once the Commander asked my department to scrutinize El Shaira's holdings, we soon uncovered dozens of damning transactions that proved without a shadow of a doubt that he was financing the most violent Muslim terror groups in the Middle East. None of this came as any great surprise. Most of A.C.T.I.O.N's intel gathering over the past few years had been clear enough for even a rookie analyst to comprehend."

Durkin stopped, took a final drag from his pipe and then began to empty its bowl in a glass ashtray on the table before him. "Then just about the time of the meeting you just saw on the wall, Arman's sister Falal began funneling large sums of money through various dummy European corporations. For a few weeks it looked like she and her brother were simply hiding their funds. But we kept digging, following this twisted trail until we hit paydirt."

Durken had removed a small jackknife from his jacket and was digging out the remains of his ashes from his pipe bowl. Sinclair admired how he was purposely pausing in his narration of the facts so as to add dramatic flare. It had to be driving the Commander bonkers. Sure enough, her boss began tapping that artificial leg of hers and once again folded her arms over her chest.

"Get on with it, Carl, we haven't got all bloody day."

Durkin winked at Sinclair and put away his pipe and jackknife. "Right, right. Commander. Sorry, I just wanted to give Agent Sinclair all the pertinent facts."

"And you've done so. Proceed."

"Yes, of course, Commander. If you'll restart the visual display, I'll continue."

The wall now showed a bustling Arab seaport. It was one Sinclair had never visited but was familiar to her from her college geography studies.

"Tripoli," Carl Durkin pointed to the busy port with all its giant transports crowding the harbor. "Arman and his sister have organized some kind of scientific expedition to be launched from there. In a period of two weeks a half dozen desert vehicles arrived here, along with several of the Middle East's most prominent archeologists: men and women considered experts in African history."

Now the video was showing several desert-ready canvas covered trucks being lifted out of the hold of a ship and set down on the docks where dozens of heavily armed men in desert gear with head scarves were waiting.

"Are those Berbers?" Sinclair asked as she studied the scene playing out before her.

"Yes," Durkin confirmed. "From Agent Porter's earlier reports, we learned that El Shaira had recruited over a hundred of these fierce desert tribesmen. The last we heard they had established a staging camp outside the city on the very fringes of the desert while the academics were staying at the posh Corinthia Bab Africa Hotel in the most modern part of the business district."

The image changed to show several distinguished looking men and women, most in western clothing, gathered in a massive lobby along with several armed guards.

The picture froze and Carl Durkin folded his hands on the table.

"These were last images we received from Agent Porter," the Commander resumed the tale for the brunette agent. "In his last radio message, Porter reported having intercepted a communiqué from El Shaira to his people back in Cairo indicating he was close to the location of 'the tree.'"

"The tree? That sounds rather cryptic. Is it some kind of code?" Sinclair's mind was working at hyper-speed, sifting through everything she'd just been told.

"We don't know," the Commander confessed. "Our code people are working on it; cross-referencing any meaning of the word with that particular locale. So far they've come up empty."

"And that was the last contact from Porter?"

"Yes. After arriving in Tripoli, he reported having hired a desert guide who knew something about the Berber's mysterious expedition. But because he disappeared so quickly, we have no way of knowing the identity of this individual or if he might have any information concerning Porter's ultimate fate.

"That, Agent Sinclair is your new assignment. You will travel to Tripoli, attempt to find this guide and learn what he told Porter."

"What about El Shaira and his desert hunt?"

The Commander started to answer but then directed her next words to Durkin. "That will be all Carl. Thank you for your report. Please have your section continue monitoring the target and inform me immediately if you learn anything new relevant to the mission."

"Yes, sir." Carl Durkin rose from his chair and nodded to Sinclair once before exiting the room.

Nicola Sinclair shifted uncomfortably in her seat as her Commander shut off the wall monitor and then glared at her.

"Listen to me and listen to me very carefully, Nicola. Your mission is to find this unknown native and learn what he knows. That is your primary objective. If you complete it successfully, you will then report your findings to this station and we'll decide what course of action must be taken next."

Sinclair twisted her chair around and looked up at the face she knew all too well.

"Am I making myself crystal clear, Agent?"

"Yes, Sir."

"I should demote you to desk-duty after that stunt you pulled in Hawaii. You're mission was to locate the poor girl and then call in the troops."

"I did that."

"Only after you single-handedly attacked and infiltrated a compound manned by a small army of terrorists. You could have gotten yourself and Miss Mulama killed. This kind of reckless disregard for protocol has to stop!"

Niki Sinclair folded her own arms in front of her and mumbled, "You're a bloody bitch, you know that, Sir."

The Commander slapped the table before her. "I told your father letting you become an A.C.T.I.O.N. agent would never work. Keep it up and you will only prove me right."

"And so now you make it personal, Mother!" Sinclair jumped to her feet unable to contain her frustration any longer. "I'm sick to death of having to tip-toe around you whenever I'm given an assignment. I am a fully trained A.C.T.I.O.N. operative and have proven my worth to this organization and time and time again.

"But it never is quite good enough for you, is it, Mother?"

"I am still your superior, Agent Sinclair. I would suggest you curb your temper and do not forget that. It would be a shame to have to discipline you for so foolish a lack of control."

Nicola Sinclair could feel the fire welling up in her veins. *The woman is bloody insufferable!* She mentally counted to ten.

"Will that be all, Commander?"

The Commander coolly waited a few seconds before replying. "Yes. Report to the Quartermaster next. I'm told they have some new toys for you to play with and then check in with Fabrications. They have a new Canadian I.D. cover for you as well as a copy of all of Porter's communiqués. Study them carefully and then destroy them. You'll be traveling to Tripoli as a history professor from McGill University. You'll fly out of Paris in twenty-four hours."

Agent Sinclair picked up her overcoat and started for the door.

"Agent Sinclair."

She turned and regarded the woman she both loved and hated in equal measure. "Yes?"

"Good luck."

Sinclair pulled open the door, walked out and slammed it shut behind her.

***

The retractable tricycle undercarriage landing gear of the Mi-24 Hind Russian helicopter popped from its belly as the ugly, olive green machine dropped out of the sky in the middle of the desert. Its top-mounted five-blade main rotor and three-bladed tail rotor both whipped the hot yellow sand into a miniature cyclone that momentarily engulfed the large gunship as if it were being swallowed whole by the arid wasteland. Then, as quickly as it has arisen, the agitated dust storm abated as the blades slowed to a gradual stop and the top-mounted turboshaft engines ceased their howling.

From the middle of the Hind five men in traditional Berber garb emerged. Each carried a Russian assault rifle, plus various blades and swords strapped to their waists over their loose fitting brown *chalwar* pants and *haik* tunics. Tan colored turbans covered most of their heads as they hurried across the soft fiery sand. Their goal was the metallic object sticking out of the ground thirty yards in front of the helicopter.

Buried over its wheel-rims was an abandoned Land Rover. Its windows were smashed out and its interior was filled with sand.

One of the five men was bigger and taller than the others. A veritable giant, he was almost seven feet tall and wore expensive wrap-around sunglasses. He was their leader and a foreigner to this inhospitable world. He was a German named Gunther Friedoff and he was a professional soldier who sold his skills to whoever had money to afford him.

"Fan out," he waved his hand over his head in a circle for his squad of Berbers. "Fifty yards to all four compass points. Fire your weapons if you find anything!" Silently the four desert warriors began jogging away from Friedoff and the buried vehicle. Watching them go, he pulled a cellular phone from an inner pocket and peeling off his sunglasses, punched in a number. He held the flat plastic monitor against his right ear and waited.

There was a soft buzz and then a familiar voice. "Yes?"

"Friedoff here. Let me speak to El Shaira."

"Hold a second."

Friedoff scratched his square chin with his sunglasses, his eyes squinting as he faced the awful glare of the desert. He was dirty, tired and hungry. Finding the Land Rover had not improved his disposition.

The phone spoke. "You found him?" Friedoff recognized El Shaira's cool, commanding voice.

"*Nein*. We found his Land Rover, but there is no sign of Porter. The Rover is half buried in the middle of nowhere."

"Please clarify. Is there an oasis near by? Mountains? Any type of topography at all?"

"All I'm seeing is a vast, empty plain in all directions. There is nothing here, Herr Shaira. I give you my word."

There was silence on the other end. Then an Arab curse followed by, "Very well. Search the vehicle carefully. Bring back anything you find in it and note the area for future reference."

The phone went silent in Friedoff's hand and he shut it off.

So much for this futile exercise. Why the Brit had driven out to this godforsaken place was beyond the mercenary's imagination but one thing was all too obvious; Alan Porter had never left it alive.

***

Seated on the lip of his Olympic-sized swimming pool, Arman El Shaira tossed the cell-phone to his personal assistant, Jacques Marceau, who stood behind him, and then dropped back into the cool water. Gunther Friedoff's report was just another dead end and the rich, powerful Arab Sheik felt his frustration begin to build up within him. Swimming was one of his many athletic pastimes that helped ease his mind and restore balance to his attitude.

With each powerful stroke, pulling the water to him, the sleek, fit, olive hued El Shaira felt the tension in his muscles slipping away. His long, lean body sliced through the water effortlessly and with each new stroke seemed to gain speed. Having been raised in a desert heavy land, the young sheik had learned to swim while attending college in London and took to it much like a proverbial fish to water. By his second year he'd not only made the swimming team but been elected its captain by his peers. This only increased the handsome young Arab's notoriety and eventually he amassed a considerable entourage made of rich young men and women from the more prestigious English families. All these contacts would later be beneficial in his many financial dealings which he used to increase his own family's wealth and power among the prosperous rich oil producing nations of the Middle East.

After another twenty minutes of pushing himself physically, El Shaira slowed his strokes and allowed his muscles to relax. Reaching the ladder at the end of the pool, he easily climbed out of the water feeling refreshed and re-energized.

Marceau, a small man with thinning gray hair and wire-rimmed glasses followed behind him as the tall, wet man marched to the exit doors of the cavernous gymnasium. There he turned around and took the white terrycloth robe the little man had been holding folded over his arm like a waiter's cloth. He slipped it on, tied the belt about his middle and brushed his jet black hair back from his forehead.

"Go back to my office and establish a video call with my sister," El Shaira said. "I'll be there once I've showered and dressed."

"Yes, Monsieur, as you wish." The efficient Mr. Marceau spun about and walked off towards the building's private elevator at the end of the hall. El Shaira continued on his way to the showers.

❋❋❋

Pan Am Flight 236 from Paris landed at the Mitiga International Airport shortly after noon and Nicola Sinclair had no problems passing through customs with her fake Canadian passport. Her visa identified her as Doctor Nicola Sinclair of McGill University in Montreal. Dressed in a smart looking green cotton dress, with flats and a pretty little brown beret, she was the picture of scholarly innocence. When asked what her purpose was for visiting Libya, she smiled innocently and replied, "I'm doing research on the archeological history of your wonderful country." The custom agent, a fat, greasy fellow merely shrugged, stamped her folder and handed it back to her without a word.

She picked up her one piece of luggage and started for the airport's exit. Mitiga was located only eight kilometers from the center of Tripoli and she could clearly see its many architectural minarets as she left the shadows of the terminal. The Tripoli International Airport had been heavily damaged during the Libyan Civil War of 2014 and was no longer in use. The heat struck her immediately and she knew it was going to take some getting used to. Like all international airports everywhere, the curb was jam-packed with private automobiles and taxis all vying to get in and out without crashing into one another.

"*Bonjour, Mademoiselle*," a young, teenage Arab boy sporting a Moroccan Fez on his head and a very thin mustache greeted her, shoving others forcefully out of his way. "You require safe and reliable transportation?" He inquired in flawless French. It was the most popular foreign language on the continent; a lasting remnant of the colonial era.

"*Oui*," Sinclair replied, making sure to use the more colloquial Canadian French rather than its root Parisian version. "I do. You have such transportation?"

The lad half-turned, bowed and swept his arm to indicate a shiny yellow low-slung French Citroen sedan. "She is Bella, my one true treasure, Allah be blessed."

Sinclair laughed softly and handed the boy her suitcase. "And what is your name, oh Master of the Beautiful Bella?"

"I am Turon Bey, Mademoiselle, at your humble service." He slapped his chest and started for the parked automobile.

"Then, be so kind as to take me to the Tripoli Radisson Blu Hotel."

He pulled open the back door and bowed again. "As Mademoiselle wishes."

***

Arman El Shaira entered his spacious office on the top floor of his privately owned office building and headed straight for his ornate, handcrafted wooden desk. He wore a five thousand dollar hand tailored silk suit and four hundred dollar Italian shoes. He was the picture of a world famous playboy, with his dark good looks masking the hawk-like intensity of his dark gray eyes.

Mr. Marceau was over in the corner by the wetbar and pointed to the upright computer laptop monitor. "Your sister is awaiting your call."

"Merci, Jacques. I will have that coffee now."

El Shaira took one glance out the window behind his desk before dropping into his leather padded chair. The panoramic view captured the bustling harbor in the distance and portions of the old ancient bazaar to the east of the city's center. Tripoli's history was one of continuous blood and warfare.

As it was, it always will be. The old desert staying surfaced in his thoughts. Despite wonders of modern science and technology, some things never change.

Marceau came over holding a demitasse of thick black, South American coffee on a small china plate. He set it down before El Shaira and then backed up to take a chair to the right of the desk.

El Shaira took a sip of the heavily caffeinated brew while punching the "send" button on his computer keyboard. Instantly the blue screen before him evaporated into the face of his beautiful younger sister. It was much like looking at a younger, female version of himself. Falal El Shaira had the same smooth olive skin, rounded cheek-bones, full lips and piercing gray eyes under narrow black lashes. He recognized her own office behind her in their family's Cairo Headquarters.

"*Salam*, Falal." There were no pleasantries between them. Both had long ago come to respect each other as equals and allies in their mutual goals to expand their financial power. What ever affection they held for each other was superfluous to their working arrangements. Each needed the other.

"Greetings, brother," she returned stoically. "Has the A.C.T.I.O.N. agent been found?"

"He vanished into the deep desert three days ago. Early this morning our people found what was left of his automobile. It was half-buried in sand with no discernible landmarks within fifty kilometers of the site."

"Then you assume he is dead?"

"That would be a logical assumption." He took another drink of coffee.

"But what of the Tree? Do you think he found it?"

El Shaira put up his palms in supplication. "Who can say? Still, we do know he spent many days questioning various scholars in the bazaar before eluding our men and disappearing.

"And why else would he have driven out to such a dangerous area alone?"

She bit her lower lip which he knew meant she was strategizing what he had just told her. Falal was a thinker and her mental prowess often impressed him with its clarity and thoroughness. Very little ever escaped his sister's scrutiny.

"And what of our own people?" she asked. "Are they any closer in deciphering the scrolls?"

"They tell me many of the entries have been re-translated over the centuries in multiple languages and their main objective is interpreting the actual writings as they were first set down. It could be weeks….maybe months before they have a location for us."

He hated relaying such a report but facts were facts. The historians they had recruited were the top experts in their field. He still felt confident they would eventually break the ancient codes and find a route to the Tree.

Falal looked at him from the monitor for a second and then her eyes seemed to glow with an unexpected thought. "Arman, consider the following. If Porter, after observing your efforts suddenly abandoned his spying and drove off into the desert then what does that suggest to you?"

"That somehow he learned of the Tree's location."

"How would that have been possible?"

"He found someone…" El Shaira sat up straight. "Someone who pointed him towards the deep desert."

"And who would this person be?"

El Shaira thought for a second then snapped his fingers. "Another scholar! Someone we do not know."

"Then I would consider learning this person's identity your top priority from this point forward."

"Agreed, Falal. If there is such a learned man here in Tripoli, surely one of our people must know of him."

"Yes. One other thing, brother."

"Yes?"

"A.C.T.I.O.N. will most certainly send someone to find Porter."

"Do not worry about that, dear sister. After his disappearance, we did locate where Porter was staying here in the city. We now have people watching his rooms. If anyone appears there, they will be dealt with accordingly."

Falal smiled. "Good, we've come too far to fail now."

***

The Tripoli Radisson Blu Hotel was in the heart of the business district called the Misrata. It was here that hundreds of foreign companies had established their offices after the U.N. imposed trade sanctions had been lifted in 2003. Now the city was a boomtown and upon entering the hotel's main lobby, Nicola Sinclair, was surrounded by people from all parts of the globe in various attire and speaking dozens of languages.

The interior décor was as posh as any European hotel she'd ever stayed in and the service was impeccable. The clerk at the registration desk greeted her in fluent French and acted as if her presence at the hotel was a personal gift to him from Allah. Sinclair could only smile at the man's jovialness.

A bellboy carried her bag and escorted her to her suite on the tenth floor where he deposited the suitcase on her giant, soft bed and then bowed politely, after she gave him a generous tip in dinars. He touched his fingertips to his lips and forehead and departed leaving her alone for the first time since arriving.

Sinclair fell back into a thickly padded easy chair in the main room, kicked off her shoes and sighed deeply. She'd told the young cabbie, Turan Bey, to come back in an hour as she would have need of his services then. He had been delighted and promised to be back at the appointed time. So she had one hour to shower, change her clothes and report back to headquarters.

She got back to her feet, went into the bedroom and began to strip. She could already imagine the relaxing feel of the warm water on her tired body.

Thirty minutes later she was wrapped in one of the hotel's soft robes, a towel wrapped around her head as her hair was still damp. She'd opened her laptop computer on the writing desk in the suite's main room and sent off an e-mail letter to her office at McGill in Montreal announcing her safe arrival. The recipient of this communiqué was an A.C.T.I.O.N. field agent who immediately re-routed it to her controller, Byron Fitzwalter back in Sleaford HQ.

Five minutes later the screen indicated a reply and she pulled it up. It read, "Good. Have located Agent Porter's rented apartment in the city. Attached is a map with coordinates. Investigate at earliest convenience. Proceed with caution. BF."

Sinclair pulled up the map, it indicated an area in the city's Old Town. She immediately synced it with her smart-phone and once done, acknowledged Byron's message as having been received and then deleted all of them from her PC.

Closing it, she looked at the modern metal clock on the wall. She had twenty minutes to dress and get down to the lobby in time to meet her young tour guide. But before she did so, she had to make a quick stop in the hotel's mini-mall and buy something for the affable young driver.

So far, all was going as planned.

***

"Here, catch!" Niki Sinclair said as she tossed the new smart-phone she had just purchased to Turan Bey, standing by his cab holding the back door open for her.

He caught it one-handed and then his eyes doubled in size when he realized what it was he was holding.

"It's for you, Turan. That way I can call you directly whenever I have need of your services."

"But Mademoiselle," he began to stammer. "It is too expensive a gift for such an unworthy person as I."

"Don't be silly," Sinclair said as she pulled out her special Rayban sunglasses and slid them over her eyes. She wore a smart, cool, light blue cotton pants suit with a matching scarf of a darker indigo. This she would wrap around her head when they reached their destination in respect of the local customs. "I am a stranger here and your helping me to get about is of invaluable assistance to me, Turan. No more arguments. Understood?'

For a second she caught herself sounding like her mother, the Commander; an unpleasant revelation at best.

"Oui, Mademoiselle," the lad nodded, smiling broadly. "*Merci beaucoup.*"

"You are welcome," she replied. "Now take me to the old town bazaar, El Medina. I wish to do some shopping."

***

As it turned out, Turan Bey was an amateur historian and the second they pulled away from the hotel's main entrance, he passionately launched into his oratory. "Did you know that Tripoli was founded in the 7th Century BC by the Phoenicians? They originally named it Oea. Due to the city's long history, there are many sites of archeological significance..."

Resting comfortably in the back seat, Sinclair relaxed and was able to drone out his friendly travelogue. She listened in silence as they drove away from the modern center of Tripoli towards the clay and mortar walls that surrounded El Medina. There were three gates that provided access to this sector and they entered through the one called Bab Al-Bahr in the northern wall. Once there, Turan Bey found a parking spot and together they started off on foot through the small narrow corridors that made up the maze-like bazaar. Sinclair noted there were as many tourists as natives filling the small streets and the noise of so many voices added to the atmosphere of the ancient bazaar. Here traditional wares such as fine jewelry and clothing could be purchased for a fair price....if the buyer were willing to haggle with the seller. It was considered good manners to argue over the price until both parties felt they'd been won a fair deal.

She bought a few trinkets of beaten silver as a camouflage should anyone be following her and curious about her activities. Her actual objective was to purchase female Bedouin clothing such as the long black robes *(abayas)*, head-scarves *(hijabs)*, face-scarves *(niquabs)* which, when worn, hid all but the wearer's eyes. She bought three complete sets and then had Turan carry them back to his Bella and lock them up in the trunk.

Done with shopping, he found them a quaint indoor restaurant and they had an early dinner of succulent lamb kabobs with ice cold sweet tea.

"You are spoiling me, Mademoiselle," Turan confessed, patting his belly as they left the eatery. "Where would you like to go now?"

"Let's just drive around," Sinclair suggested. "I'm told the old Italian Red Castle is still standing and perhaps we could go past the National Museum."

The sky was turning purple with twilight and she needed to scout out the area where Porter's rented apartment was located. From the map Byron had sent her, she knew it was in on a street directly between the two sites he had mentioned.

Minutes later, they were rolling through the city with the young driver once again verbally relating other historical facts. All the while, Sinclair, in the back seat, had rolled down her window and was using the special mini-camera in her glasses to record the streets and buildings they passed. When they stopped at a busy intersection only a block away from Porter's place, she had a direct view and took half a dozen pictures.

Having what she'd come for, Sinclair told her new friend she was tired and to take her back to the hotel. Once there, she would study the layout she'd captured with her spy camera, set out her clothing and gear and then try to get some sleep.

For Lady Action, her mission wouldn't begin until after midnight.

***

Dressed in her newly purchased Arab clothing, Nicola Sinclair took the stairs down to the first floor and exited out of the hotel's back door as not to be seen. It was after two in the morning and as she moved through the back alleyway, she relished the quiet all around her. She'd purposely chosen the dark robe and scarves so that as long as she stayed within the stygian blackness of the small side streets, she was all but invisible; a flitting shadow moving from one place to another.

The night air was a welcome relief after the day's stifling heat and she could just barely smell the ocean brine from the harbor to the north. Occasionally a city bus or police vehicle would appear and she'd immediately duck into the nearest alley or shop front alcove. A single woman walking the streets at this hour would be stopped and questioned. The only females to do so were prostitutes and they generally congregated near the expensive international hotels or the local bars. Just another reason why she was glad Agent Porter had rented rooms in Old Town.

Thanks to Byron Fitzwalter's map and her earlier excursion into the city, Sinclair was able to memorize the shortest, best route to her target. It took her less than two hours to reach the old three story building set in the neighborhood just behind the huge National Museum. Sliding along a rough brick wall, she peered at it from the corner. There was a commotion across the street and she watched as a mangy tomcat suddenly bolted from a tiny alley chasing after several big rats. She waited to see if their noise would attract any of the inhabitants of the surrounding buildings. Above her all the windows were darkened as families slept peacefully in their beds.

She dashed across the street and disappeared into the narrow alley. Dodging fallen trash cans, she made her way to a small, cramped back yard. Above her dozens of clothes lines crisscrossed each other like a complicated giant spider's web. Clothing of every type and size draped from many of these sagging lines.

Sinclair spotted the second story window she was looking for. A tiny balcony jutted out from it and she estimated it's height to be twenty-feet from the ground. Hurriedly she peeled off her cumbersome outer garments and stuffed them into a backpack she'd worn beneath them. She set it down behind several trash bins. Beneath the Arab outfit she wore a one piece, black jumpsuit with a tight hood she hastily pulled over her head. On her feet were light weight boat-shoes with rubber soles. Velcro sealing pockets were sewn on both thighs of her suit and arms, each containing tiny tools to aid in her search. Strapped to her belt at the small of her back was a holster containing an A.C.T.I.O.N. pistol model P-45 called a Pea-Shooter; a unique handgun created by the gunsmiths back at Sleaford. It was a small automatic pistol that looked like a tiny .22 but fired .45 caliber bullets from a four round magazine; easy to conceal but having the reliable stopping power of a larger gun. She appreciated the purpose of the weapon but hated how, when fired, its recoil kicked like a mule.

She quickly grabbed several trash cans, secured their lids and moved them so that they were just under the tiny square balcony. Then she jogged back down the alleyway a few yards and readied herself. As a young girl, Sinclair had been a formidable athlete and excelled at gymnastics. It was a skill she continued to practice finding it extremely useful in many of her missions like this one. She took several shallow breaths, folded into a crouched ready position and then started running.

Her gait was fast and relaxed and just as she neared the trash cans she leaped forward, landed on them and her body sprang upwards. Her arms reached out, caught the edge of the balcony and with graceful ease she flew up over the railing to land catlike on the flimsy, wooden platform. It creaked under her weight and her eyes hastily scanned the windows above, below and across the alley. All remained still indicating no one had heard her.

Sighing, she turned her attention to the window and was pleasantly surprised to see it was open by a few inches at the bottom. Considering the average temperatures, she had no problem accepting that Porter would have left it as such. Most of these old buildings had no modern air conditioning and their only way of dealing with the oppressive heat were electrical ceiling fans…and open windows.

Sinclair's gloved hands reached under the sill and carefully raised the window up. She twisted her body around and climbed into the darkened room.

There was just enough light from the widow to show her she was in a small bedroom containing a single bed, two end tables to either side, a bureau with a mirror top and a closet with its door open. There were two doors, both opened. Sinclair paused, slid her special sunglasses from one of her hip pockets and adjusted them over her eyes turning on the infra-red vision. Instantly she was looking at a surreal green world and could see the door on the other side of the bed led to a tiny bathroom and the one to her immediate right went out into a larger kitchen/living room area. Ignoring that for the moment, she skirted the bed and went to the bureau. The top was littered with a maps of the city and surrounding locales plus menus from restaurants throughout Tripoli. Porter obviously enjoyed eating out.

She then meticulously began going through the three drawers hoping to find any kind of clue that would lead her to the contact Porter had established. But all she found was neatly folded clothing; mostly warm weather stuff. Next she went at the closet. Hanging up were several pairs of pants and shirts, along with a sports jacket. On the floor was an old Army duffel bag which she hoisted onto the bed and searched. In this she found Porter's personal arsenal made up of several pistols snug in their leather holsters, extra ammunition clips and three sharp knives of various lengths and styles. Knowing he could never have brought these through customs, she had to assume his unknown ally had provided him with the arms.

As she zipped the canvas bag shut, her trained instincts felt a familiar unease. Although it appeared as if no one had been in the room since Porter's departure, she had the gut hunch that she was not the first person to be searching through his belongings. Someone else had preceded her and done such a professional job of it, there were no obvious signs of their having done so.

All of it was just instinct; the instinct she'd been trained to believe and trust.

This factor immediately increased the immediate threat level she faced. If others had already searched these quarters then it was a safe bet they might return. Either that or they were keeping the building under surveillance. She felt her stomach muscles tighten and as she entered the larger of the two rooms, she reached behind her back and pulled the Peashooter free of its holster.

The main room was twice the size of the bedroom and bathroom combined; a square living area with a few pieces of worn furniture set around a thick woven rug on the floor. There was a small sofa and two threadbare chairs facing a scarred wooden coffee table separating them. Beyond these were a stove against the back wall, a tiny sink and counter and a portable ice box on the floor in the corner. To her left as she walked past was the door to the hall and then a small writing desk and swivel chair.

Gripping her pistol tightly, she looked down at the desk top buried under newspapers and tourist fliers. It had one drawer to the right and she examined this as well. It was empty except for a few pencils, pens and paper clips. Over the desk, tacked to the wall was a calendar displaying the picture of the bazaar at El Medina. As she studied it words painted in white slowly began to emerge from the image and she realized they'd been written with some kind of ink visible only to special lenses like her own infrared Raybans. She tapped the temple of her glasses with her free hand and recorded what she was seeing. The lettering was Arabic and she had no idea what it meant.

Then she heard a footstep just outside the door.

Sinclair spun about and dropped in a crouch behind the desk.

The front door smashed inward having been kicked by a heavy combat boot.

Its owner, a Berber, charged into the room spraying bullets everywhere as he clutched a short German machine-gun in his hands. The bullets tore through the walls and furniture in a deafening rain of destruction. The big Arab was followed by another desert warrior carrying his own submachine gun.

Sinclair, still on one knee, shot the second one in the head and he dropped back against the open door. Unaware his partner had been shot, the first attacker stood flatfooted trying to see if his salvo had hit anything alive. He said something Arabic which Sinclair took to mean, "Turn on the lights."

Which was when she shot him in the chest sending his body flying backwards; his weapon spinning off in another direction.

Suddenly a third Berber assassin dove into the room firing his weapon adding to the loud confusion of the ill planned attack. Sinclair dropped her head as chunks of the wall dropped on her shoulders. The Berber spun around in a circle, his shots creating a deadly field that encompassed the entire room. A dim light from the hallway's overhead bulbs painted the frantic killer in sharp relief.

Then his machine gun clicked empty and he stood momentarily perplexed looking down at it. Smoke wafted up from the hot barrel.

Sinclair rose up, shook herself free of the dust and plaster that covered her head and shoulders, leveled her gun in a two handed grip and blew him away. He fell back screaming into the first gunmen.

It was time to get the hell out of there. She jumped over the body by the door and into the hall. To her left she saw more armed Berbers rushing up the stairs from the first floor. She aimed and fired. The lead man's head jerked back as blood and gore exploded from the back his head. He fell into his comrades who did their best to catch him.

Meanwhile Sinclair re-holstered her Peashooter and then reached into one of the pouches on her utility belt. From it she pulled a handful of glass balls the size of children's marbles. She tossed them at the Berbers and then turned and started running away in the opposite direction. As she did so, she tore off her sunglasses and put them back in her shoulder pocket.

The flash-bang balls all exploded simultaneously behind her and she smiled at the cries of her enemies as the bright, liquid phosphorous exploded in a blinding white light. It would be minutes before they regained their sight. Ahead was the stairwell to the top floor and the roof. As she took the stairs two at a time, she once again grabbed her custom-made handgun, ejected the spent clip and added a new one she'd taken from the thigh pocket on her left leg. She held it before her aimed upward fully aware that other residents might appear and accidentally get caught in the middle of this firefight.

No sooner as she had the thought than a door on the third floor popped open and a disheveled man stuck his head out. Passing him, Sinclair could see the face of his frightened wife hiding behind him.

"*Laa onzor*!" she warned using what few Arabic words she knew that loosely translated to "No look." At the same time she indicated her pistol. The man's eyes widened and he quickly shoved his wife back and closed the door. Looking down the corridor, Sinclair saw others doing the same thing. Having heard what they recognized as gunshots, these people had no intention of letting their curiosity get the best of them.

***

Gunther Friedoff pushed through his men who were still trying to clear their eyes as he stomped up the stairs to the second floor.

"*Bewegen*!" he barked. "Move! Get out of my way!" He saw the dead man on the landing with half his head missing and stepped over him. "And get rid of this worthless piece of trash," he said pointing to the body.

As he marched along the tight hallway, he once again wished he could have recruited more of his fellow Germans after El Shaira had first hired him three years earlier. Instead part of his duties were to train the desert dwellers and make them an effective quick-response fighting unit. For the most part he'd succeeded but when it came to urban battle as they were now tasked with, the outcome was always in doubt. Berbers hated city dwelling and moving about in their bulky robes and turbans proved to be a serious impediment in such close quarters.

Friedoff stopped at the ruined door to Alan Porter's flat and smoothly drew his own Desert Eagle .45 automatic before entering. Seeing it was still dark, his left hand went up and found the light switch. What he beheld was the aftermath of a bloody encounter that had left three of his men dead on the floor and the room looking like a tornado had torn it apart. He carefully checked the bedroom; saw that it was empty and hastily returned to the hall where his men were awaiting him. Their sight had returned and one of them pointed his finger up to indicate where their prey had fled to.

"Come! The bitch mustn't be allowed to escape!"

***

Sinclair charged up the stairs to the roof hoping she could evade her pursuers by fleeing over the rooftops. These buildings were constructed so close together it would be easy enough to jump from on to another.

She burst out of the door at the top of the stairs only to collide with a huge Berber who had been in the process of reaching for the doorknob. Through the slit in his turban, she saw the surprise reflected in his eyes. She also noted there were two others right behind the man she stood toe to toe with.

Sinclair brought her head down hard, butting it into the man's covered face and smashed his nose. She heard the crack and then his scream of pain. He instinctively fell back bringing up his hands; hands that held a machine-gun. Sinclair kicked him in the groin and now he was bending forward. She clubbed the back of his head with her pistol and then aimed it at the next Berber and shot that one in the chest.

Two down and one to go.

The man she had kneed had dropped in front of her and as she sidestepped to avoid his falling into her, she looked up in time to see the third warrior coming at her screaming at the top of his lungs with a curved Arab scimitar aimed at her head. She ducked as the blade whistled over her head missing it by mere inches. Sinclair pushed herself forward and tackled the Berber about the stomach and both of them went down onto the rough tar-paper that covered the roof.

Before the fellow could recover, she rolled away from him just as his arm swung out with the blade a second time. It hit the roof-tiles missing her a second time. Sinclair came up on one knee and shot him in the head. The sword fell from his lifeless fingers as his arm dropped.

Back on her feet, she started running to get as far away from the door as possible. The flat roof was littered with all kinds of odds and ends from boxes, crates and discarded appliances. The debris of apartment dweller, anything people no longer wanted ended up stored there. Most of it was junk but it still proved a formidable obstacle course for her to cross as he headed for the edge and the next roof.

She heard angry yelling voices behind her and kept running. Then gunshots banged away and she knew they were all aimed at her. It only made her run faster. Several crates she ran past exploded as several bullets hit them and dozens of tiny, sharp shards showered her. She kept her head down holding up her gunhand to shield it from the shrapnel.

Then she was at the end of the roof and happy to see it was skirted by a two foot ledge. She leaped onto this and over the divide between buildings which was no more than three yards across. Landing on her feet, she just kept running.

Part of her path over this second roof brought her near the street side and as she rushed along she was unaware she was being followed from below. That became clear when a chunk of the ledge below suddenly blew up sending pieces of brick and mortar spraying out over the area behind here. The noise was deafening and made her ears ring. Taking a quick look down over the ledge, she saw another half dozen of her foes on foot racing along the street, two were hefting rifles outfitted with R.P.Gs (rocket-propelled-grenades).

One of them looked up and spotted her. He yelled to his mates, stopped and pointed his rifle in her direction.

Sinclair bolted away from the edge and started running again just as he fired. His round missile flew up onto the roof, bounced off a packing crate and rolled towards where she had just been standing. When it went off, Sinclair was only a few yards ahead of it and the concussion blast hit her back with the force of a Mack truck. It knocked her into the air and over the ledge.

That's just not fair! She thought as she was flung into the sky. Her arms outstretched she began to fall to the pavement below sure she would either break her back or neck. She did her best to hang on to the Peashooter still in her right hand as he fell backwards.

Then her body hit the dozens of clotheslines extending over the street from buildings to either side and much to her amazed surprise she bounced up from them.

In mid-bounce Sinclair managed to twist her head about and realize what it was that had saved her from slamming into the street. But now she was falling again and once more hit the lines of rope. This time there was no bouncing from them and they only stopped her descent for a brief second before the weight of her body slipped through them. She dropped another ten feet onto a second level of lines shaking up the many items of clothing hung from them. Regaining some semblance of control, Nicola Sinclair twisted her body around completely so when she again slipped the man-made web of ropes, she was falling face first towards the final set of clotheslines.

Somewhere below them were the Berbers. She glimpsed two of them rushing just below her as she dropped onto the taut ropes. It was her hope they hadn't seen her topple off the roof and by their movements she knew they had lost sight of her. It was her one advantage she had to make use of; a final element of surprise.

She hooked her left arm around a clothesline holding up a long white sheet so as to swing down like a pendulum directly behind the two men she'd seen. Feet out, she hit them both in the back and sent them sprawling into the ground. Then, before they could see what had hit them, she dropped to the pavement and shot them both. There was movement behind her and she turned just as the man with the rifle struck her across the side of her head with the butt of his weapon.

Sinclair fell hard with stars swimming in her head. Lying on her side at his feet, she tried to bring up her pistol but her assailant wouldn't give her the chance. He stepped on her chest with a booted foot shoving her down and then began to bring the rifle down on her head for a killing blow.

There was a loud shot and the man's swing ended abruptly as his entire body jerked upright. A second gunshot followed the first and the Berber keeled over to hit the ground beside her dead.

Then she heard a loud motor and looking up, saw a man come racing up on a motorcycle. He brought the bike to a skidding stop before her and looking down at her said, "Hurry up and get on!"

Sinclair tried her best to focus but her vision was blurred from the hit to the head she'd taken. With her last remaining ounce of strength, she managed to get to her feet, her free hand reached to the rider. He held it firmly and pulled her up to him. Then he allowed her throw her leg over the back of the seat and settled in behind her. She put her pistol away and wrapped both arms around his middle. She noted his body seemed trim and fit and putting her head against his back she felt the coolness of a smooth leather jacket.

"Hold on!" he ordered said in perfect English as he twisted the gas handle.

The big bike roared again, the rider brought it about pivoting on his left leg and then let it rip. The machine shot forward and Sinclair had all she could do to hang on. The wind felt good against her cheek as they fled the area and raced to safety.

***

Gunther Friedoff watched the pair on the big motorcycle drive off into the night, his men beside him on the roof firing futilely at the escaping couple.

"*Halten*!" he cried out. "Don't waste your bullets!"

As the quiet returned, he turned away from the ledge and silently cursed. Now he had to report his failure to El Shaira. Sometimes even the obscene amount of money he was paid wasn't enough for the humiliation he endured.

Angrily he ordered his men to clean up the battlefield and remove their dead. All the while he vowed to himself he would find the woman who had inflicted such damage and she would be made to suffer before she died.

***

Nicola Sinclair kept falling in and out of sleep losing all sense of time. Images flicked through her mind like wispy shadows all making a chain of experiences she couldn't hold on to. A race through a warren of deserted streets, her clinging half-awake to her mysterious savior. Then being carried bodily across a room filled with weird machinery and deposited ever so gently onto a rough cot padded with rough-hair blankets.

And then the light came and it hurt her eyes even closed.

It was followed closely by the rat-tat-tat of machine guns pounding away directly over her head. Sinclair groaned and covered both her ears to keep the awful noise from drilling into her head.

She opened her eyes slowly only to have them flooded with blurred images. She closed them and took a deep breath. She had to calm herself down, lower her own blood pressure and regain some composure. Instinctively she knew she was in a strange place and until she knew where that was and more importantly who had brought here there, things had to be taken one step at a time.

Again her eyelids raised and now she was able to differentiate what she was actually seeing. She was in a shop of some kind, open and cluttered with all manner of machine tools from lathes, to welding torches and engine hoists. Shelves along the dirty walls were crammed with parts of various sizes and purposes. Above the one across from her was a tall window with dirty streaked panes enough to slightly diffuse the light that was bathing her face.

She brought a hand up to her head and realized someone had peeled off her hood and removed her shoes from her feet. The weight of the Peashooter was also gone from its holster at the small of her back.

In front of the shelf was a motorbike resting on its kickstand. She squinted enough to see it was a BSA Spitfire Hornet and identified it as a 1967 model by its dark Cherokee Red color. It was a very powerful desert racer that had been sold primarily in the U.S. before it was discontinued. She assumed it was the machine that she'd been a passenger on and that impressed her. It told her something about the rider; that he knew a quality machine and how to ride it.

She groaned again and rolled over to her other side to avoid the light.

"Ah, good, you're awake," said the tall man standing ten feet away by a table and chair. He had a plastic container in his hands and was dropping two white pills into the palm of his calloused left hand. Then he reached down for a cup of water and turned to face her. "Here, take these. They're for your head. You took a nasty blow."

Her rescuer was a tall man, maybe six feet-two, wearing heaving black boots, the type with reinforced steel toes, dirty dungarees, a leather belt with a heavy silver buckle that encircled a trim waist and a dark-blue tee-shirt, also soiled, which showed off his well-muscled torso. He had a broad chest and two powerfully sculptured arms that were evidence of either long years of hard labor or even more hours in a fitness gym. Sinclair guessed the former as there was nothing about this man that even hinted at an easy life of luxury but rather one of struggles and hardships.

His skin was a rich cocoa color with a bronze tan to it. He wore a neatly trimmed black goatee and mustache that gave him a devilish appearance. His mouth and nose were patrician, almost Roman in feature, and his eyes were dark and piercing under narrow brows used to squinting often. She could see the slight wrinkles which also argued a life lived outdoors in the open under the harsh African sun. Finally he had a mop of curly black hair which he wore in western fashion with neatly cut edges behind his ears and at the back of his thick neck. There, Sinclair made out a tiny silver cross descending beneath the shirt to hide whatever dangled from it.

Great. I've escaped one Berber only to be caught by another.

As he approached, she tried to rise up on her elbows only to have the room suddenly flip over in her head and she dropped back down with a gasp.

"Not so fast," the man cautioned. He crouched over her slowly and offered up the water and pills. "You'll only make yourself sick."

Looking up, Sinclair blinked and spoke at last. "Right. Thanks." Her hand reached up and he passed the pills to her. After she'd popped them in her mouth, the tall man knelt next to her, gently raised her head from behind and brought the cup to her dry lips. She took a long swallow and then pulled her head back.

"Good, now lay back for a few minutes," her host advised in a strong and pleasant voice. She couldn't quite place his accent though she thought there were some strong English influences in how he shaped his words. "Once the pills start working, you should be okay to sit up and have something to eat."

"Thanks...again. Just who the bloody hell are you?'

"Hahaahaha," the man laughed as he sat back on the cement floor, put the cup aside and crossed his legs together. This close, Sinclair saw his eyes were bright clear like chocolate diamonds. "You'll please forgive this uncouth desert son his lack of proper manners, my dear Lady Action." He kissed his fingertips and touched his forehead with a flourish. "I am the one, the only, Gordon Ari Bin Starkill."

"How do you know my codename? Wait!" She snapped her fingers and pointed at Bin Starkill. "You're Porter's secret contact!"

"Being Alan Porter's friend and ally was my great honor, Lady Action."

"But then you know what happened to him. Yes?"

"I'm afraid not. If you knew Alan at all, you know how impetuous he was. Part of my work for him was to learn the purpose of Armin El Shaira's assembled expedition and its ultimate purpose. To learn what it is they are seeking in the Deep Desert."

Bin Starkill bowed his eyes. "To my regret I was unable ascertain that information and Alan grew impatient with me."

"What happened?"

"He came to me last week saying he found another Libyan scholar who might be able to help him and that he was going to go and confer with him. That was the last I heard of him."

"Then you really don't know if he's alive or dead?" Sinclair felt some of her equilibrium and strength returning.

"Sadly, I learned, through various sources, that El Shaira's people, led by a German mercenary named Gunther Friedoff, found what was left of Alan's Land Rover buried in the sands of the Deep Desert only a few days ago. There were no signs of Porter anywhere."

"So who was this scholar he went to see?"

Starkill put his hands out palms up. "Who can say? What I do know is that El Shaira has among his party the top African historians and archeologists and as yet they have no idea where to locate the treasure he is seeking...or else they would have left their camp by now. Instead they spend their days going over ancient scrolls and old maps of the Deep Desert."

"You seem to know a great deal about their routines." Sinclair took a breath and managed to push herself up off the cot into a sitting position so that now she was on the same eye-to-eye level with Bin Starkill.

"I'm a spy...like you. It's what we do, is it not?"

Sinclair prided herself on being able to read people but she'd been a secret agent long enough to know anyone could be taught to lie like an expert. Still there was something about the handsome brown face before her that felt honest to her. Again, she was listening to her instincts. The inescapable logic said that had Bin Starkill been her enemy, he wouldn't have bothered to rescue her in the first place. Instead of this noisy, crowed shack, she would have awakened in a prison cell.

If she would have awakened at all, that was. The Berbers she had fought the night before were clearly looking to capture her. It was all too clear they had wanted her dead.

When her stocking feet hit the hard cement floor, she looked down and to her left saw her sneakers and resting atop them was her Peashooter in its detachable leather holster.

"I removed them after laying you on the cot," Bin Starkill explained seeing where she was looking. "I thought you'd sleep better without them on."

Sinclair nodded slightly. "Yes. Thank you. There is still much I don't understand."

"Understandable. Are you at all hungry?"

For the first time Nicola Sinclair felt her stomach rumble slightly and tried to remember the last time she'd actually eaten. It had been the late lunch in the bazaar at El Median with Turon Bey. "Yes, I could eat something along about now."

"Good, the headache tablets must be working." Bin Starkill jumped to his feet and went to a portable icebox set against the back wall behind the table. "I'm afraid all I've got is some goat-cheese, flatbread and dates."

"That will do quite nicely," Sinclair said touching the side of her head where she'd been clubbed by the rifle butt with her fingertips. It was still plenty sore and she could easily imagine the bruise hidden beneath her thick black hair. Thankfully, as her mother always pointed, she had a hard head and the blow hadn't done more damage. Another strike in the same place could have easily fractured her skull.

"Where exactly are we?" she asked after he'd handed her the plate and refilled her cup with more water.

"This is the back room of a very busy transport machine shop," he waved his hands about and to a door against the one wall with no windows. "We're in the middle of the harbor district with the major shipping piers beyond that door and through the main working area. The company employs a hundred machinists who are generally kept busy around the clock."

"I was wondering what was making all that noise," she grimaced while chewing on a piece of cheese. "I guess it's as good a hideaway as any, I suppose."

"Well, it also helps that the shop foreman is a cousin-twice removed," Bin Starkill grinned. "He thinks I'm a smuggler hiding from the law. And here in Tripoli the police are worse than the criminals. Family protects family, it is the way of the Taureg."

"Taureg?"

"Nomadic desert dwellers. I was brought up amongst the dunes of the mighty Sahara."

"Oh, like Berbers."

Bin Starkill turned and spat on the floor. "Do not insult me by comparing me to those farmers and camel herders. They are nothing like my people. The fact that they sell themselves to people like El Shaira proves they have no true love of the desert sands."

"My apologies," Sinclair interjected. "I meant no insult and I am most grateful for what you did last night. But..."

"You have many more questions?" he finished for her.

"Wouldn't you?"

"Then ask and I will answer...to the best of abilities to do so."

"All right. First of all, for someone raised among nomads, you speak like an educated man. Who exactly are you, Mr. Bin Starkill? And why should I trust you, aside from the fact that you saved my life last night."

"I said I was of the Taureg which is true, but my father was a British historian at Cambridge University. He met my mother, a tribal princess, on one of his many trips around the world; they fell in love and were married. At first my mother was content to leave her people and follow my father back to England. But after I was born, her heart began to ache for the hot sun and the vast emptiness of the Deep Desert.

"In the end, my parents compromised. My mother would return to her people and I would spend all my summers with her. Then in the autumn, I would return to my father to receive a proper British education. Thus for the first twenty years of my life, I was nurtured by two very different cultures."

Sinclair finished her cheese and took a drink of water. She wiped her lips with the back of her hand.

"It sounds like a remarkable upbringing, Mr. Starkill..."

"Ari, please. If we are going to be allies, we should also be friends."

"Hmm, right. But you've yet to tell me who you are working for....Ari? It's obvious you are an espionage agent but for who?"

Bin Starkill reached up and tugged the necklace draped around his neck so that the medal that had been concealed by his tee-shirt was now revealed. It was a silver-plated crucifix behind which was a starburst where the tines met at the center. Sinclair recognized it immediately.

"*Spada di Cristo*," she said in Italian. "The Sword of Christ."

"Bravo, Lady Action. Indeed. You see, I am an agent of the Pope and Holy Roman Catholic Church."

***

The campsite on the southern outskirts of the Tripoli resembled an old World War II military base camp. It was laid out in a square grid, with the larger conference tents at its center and the smaller, barracks tents surrounding those. A motor-pool had been established just beyond the tents and was made up of a dozen heavy-duty jeeps and desert vehicles that rode on tank-like treads. Hundreds of armed Berber soldiers moved about the camp in a carefree attitude while civilian experts dashed from one tent to another like busy work bees carrying maps and scrolls doing their best to stay out of the brutally hot sun that beat down on them. This far from the harbor, the cooling sea breeze was non-existent.

In the largest tent, Arman El Shaira was huddled over a huge table diorama of the Libyan Desert conversing with top scientists. Their leader was a bearded Yugoslavian named Prof. Anlo Pareen. At the moment he was anything but happy.

"I tell you, El Shaira, what you ask of us is impossible," he said throwing his hands up in the air for the umpteenth time in so many days. He pushed several other archeologists out of the way as he circled the massive diorama while pointing at its biggest feature, the giant, shapeless center of sand. "Thousands of acres of empty wasteland! It is a vast bottomless pool of nothing according to even our best satellite maps. As it has been for millions of years. And yet to ask us to find one specific place to which you have no reliable longitude or latitude nor any concrete idea of its geographic features!"

El Shaira had allowed Pareen his daily rantings in respect for his place in the academic world. Had he not been the leading expert on African archeology, the financial mogul would have had him severely beaten for his ill-mannered behavior. But he needed the man and so El Shaira did his best to placate him.

Wearing riding boots, khaki shorts and a matching shirt, El Shaira stood with his hands folded calmly behind his back and waited until Prof. Pareen ran out of steam.

"And yet an untrained British spy managed to do exactly that," he spoke coolly, his gray eyes spearing Pareen with their intensity. "Now, how do you think he managed that, my dear Professor?"

"You know this for a fact?' Pareen retorted quickly. "I was told only that the man's motor car had been found…and in an area as barren as the rest of that infernal hellhole."

"The point is, Professor, Alan Porter must have had a definitive map-point to draw him there. A map-point you and your people have yet to uncover."

"On that we are agreed," the frustrated archeologist admitted. "It is exactly what my colleagues have been searching for in hundreds of documents you have provided us with. One single clue, one sentence that will fix a set point." Pareen threw his hands up in the air again. "Without out such a direction, we could search until the end of time and never come anywhere near our target."

"Understood." El Shaira unfolded his arms keeping them at his side and dismissed Pareen with a parting command. "Keep looking."

He spun on his heels and exited the tent's open front where Gunther Friedoff stood awaiting him. The big German handed his employer a brimmed kepi hat, the style made popular by the French with the cloth tailing to shade the wearer's neck. From his shirt front pocket, El Shaira produced a pair of aviation sunglasses and put them over his eyes before accepting the cap and adjusting it on his head.

"Any word from Monsieur Marceau?"

Friedoff began to reply when El Shaira spotted his personal assistant approaching them. His clothes spotless and pristine, the flamboyant Frenchmen hated venturing outdoors and the disdain on his face as he twisted in and around the Berber troops was all too evident. He wore a stylish wide-brimmed fedora to block the sun from his white, pinched face. He was carrying his ever-present black leather briefcase pressed against his side with his left hand and when he saw El Shaira he brightened and hastened his pace.

"Jacques, tell me you have good news for me? That would be a welcome change." That last bit was directed at Friedoff who bristled at the insult but wisely kept his mouth shut.

"I believe so," Marceau replied as he began to open his briefcase. He reached in and took out three large color photographs and handed them to his boss. "From Herr Friedoff's description of the woman they encountered last evening, I did a search for any foreign females matching her body type who would have arrived in Tripoli within the past two days.

"The first two photos you are holding were taken at the airport early yesterday morning. The woman in them was listed on the incoming flight from Paris as a Canadian by the name of Nicola Sinclair who is here on a study visa from McGill University in Montreal."

The first picture El Shaira studied had been taken from an overhead security camera and showed an attractive young brunette making her way across the terminal having passed through customs. The second photo was a closer image of the same woman. From it he guessed her age to be in her mid-twenties.

"She registered herself into the Radisson Blu Hotel," Marceau continued his report. "I had calls put into one of our people in Canada and learned that there is such a name on the faculty roster, but no one has ever met this teacher face to face."

"So," El Shaira nodded, "this must be the A.C.T.I.O.N. agent we had been expecting. Send some of our people to pick her up at once."

Jacques Marceau made an embarrassed coughing noise. "Assuming that would be your wish, I already dispatched a team to the hotel. She was gone and her rooms empty of any of her belongings."

"Damn it! Am I to be constantly cursed with failures for some unfathomable reason of the fates?" El Shaira had pulled the third picture as he was cussing and Gunther Friedoff saw something in it that he recognized.

"Excuse me, El Shaira," he pointed to that last picture and then turned to Marceau. "That last picture, where was it taken?"

Marceau pushed his wire-rim glasses up on his nose and leaned forward to see which picture Friedoff was referring to. "Ah, that one was taken by the outdoor security camera at the hotel's front entrance."

El Shaira saw the woman called Nicola Sinclair getting into a yellow taxi-cab as a young Arab driver held the door open for her.

He glared at Friedoff. "Well? What is significant about this one?"

"I know that yellow cab!" Friedoff blurted, pointing at the picture. "I've seen it around the city often. It's the only one like it on the streets."

Armin El Shaira accepted Friedoff's claim and then slapped the photo into the German's hands angrily. "Then find it! And the woman! And this time I want no excuses!"

***

"Would you believe me if I told you the Church maintains secret service?" Gordon Ari Bin Starkill asked Sinclair after showing her his sacred medallion.

"As what, some kind of intelligence arm of the Swiss Guard?"

Bin Starkill clapped his hands. "Exactly! Many years ago, when certain ancient antiquities began to appear on the black market, the Holy See worried that one day certain religious artifacts would become prey to these unscrupulous traders of the world's lost histories. Thus the Pope created a secret branch of the Guard and named it the *Ombra della Croce*; Shadow of the Cross."

Sinclair, having finished her repast, set the empty platter beside her on the cot. "Say I buy any of this, Ari. How did you become one of their agents? Your personal background hardly seems like it would have put you on such a career path."

Bin Starkill laughed. "How true. And yet the circumstances were not all that out of the ordinary. You see, while at Cambridge, I majored in History and World Religions. During my final year of studies, one of my advisors suggested I go to Rome and work there on my graduation dissertation."

"Are you even Catholic?" Sinclair interrupted.

"Ha, not quite. My father is Lutheran and my mother is a Moslem. Maybe it was that very diversity that fascinated me enough to study the subject in the first place. Regardless, while at the Vatican I became friends with the Papal Librarian, Bishop Ansatore. We became close friends and it was he who eventually recruited me to join their organization."

"And you didn't feel any personal conflict becoming a spy for one of the world's most powerful religious organizations?"

"Conflict? Ah, I see what you mean. No, Miss Sinclair, the goal of the Ombra della Croce is to protect all the ancient treasures of man's history, regardless of their culture. In fact some of our people were responsible in discovering the sites of several pagan Celtic altars in Northern England and had them declared Historical Landmarks so that they would be preserved for future generations to visit and study."

Before Sinclair could ask how it was he knew her real name, there was a loud knocking on the heavy steel back door. In a split second, she'd drawn her Peashooter from its holster and was standing with it aimed at that portal.

"Easy," Bin Starkill cautioned, almost having fallen on his backside when she sprung to her feet. He rose up and hurried to the door, unhooked the latch and slid it open.

"How did it go?" he inquired of their caller.

"I was just in time," Turon Bey said as he stepped into the room carrying Sinclair's traveling luggage. "El Shaira's men were just entering the hotel's front lobby as I was going out a side door. I'm sure they didn't see me."

Niki Sinclair lowered her pistol at the sight of her young friend though a new puzzled expression appeared on her face. "Turon Bey?" She looked from the lad to Bin Starkill and then it all made sense. "You two work together!"

"But of course," Bin Starkill concurred, slapping the boy on the back. "Turon is invaluable to me. In fact it was he who brought Alan to me when he first arrived in Tripoli."

Sinclair nodded knowingly. "And your approaching me at the airport yesterday was no accident."

"My apologies for the subterfuge, Mademoiselle," Turon Bey bowed slightly. "Ari had told me Alan Porter's people would likely send someone and I was to look for any foreign ladies who traveled alone." Turon Bay moved past Sinclair and dropped her suitcase on the cot.

Bin Starkill picked up the story. "After dropping you off at the hotel, Turon called me and when he described you, I was fairly confident you were the famous Lady Action Alan had told me about."

"So all the while he was showing me around, he was reporting back to you?"

"Yes," Bin Starkill confessed. "When he told me you'd asked to see the museum district, I suspected it was because you wanted to see where Alan had stayed and that you were planning to return and the search place."

"Which is why you were nearby to save my skin when El Shaira's men almost caught me."

"Not just his men, but his chief butcher, a German mercenary named Gunther Friedoff."

Sinclair looked at her new allies and folded her arms over her chest, mulling over everything she'd been told. Finally, she spoke. "You two are really quite remarkable. But you still haven't told me what this is really all about. What is it El Shaira is so obsessed to find out there in the desert?"

"The Tree of Life," Bin Starkill said.

"Hmmm. One of Porter's last messages to A.C.T.I.O.N. headquarters had mentioned something about a tree. What is it exactly?"

"Before answering that, may I ask you a question?" Bin Starkill asked.

"What?"

"Did you find anything of worth in Alan's apartment? Anything out of the ordinary?"

Sinclair was going to say no but then remembered what she'd discovered a second before Porter's rooms had been invaded by El Shaira's Berbers. "Wait! There was something."

She reached into the pocket of her jumpsuit on the right leg and withdrew her special sunglasses. Holding them up, she pressed the temples in a particular sequence and the lenses became a monitor. With each click they pulled up the pictures she'd taken while examining Alan Porter's quarters.

"Here," she turned the glasses around so that Bin Starkill and Turon Bey could see the last picture she's snapped. "My infrared lenses found a hidden word on this calendar. It's in Arabic. Do either of you know what it means?"

Both men stepped closer scrutinized the image, which her glasses had inverted into a negative plate so that the invisible wording was clearly visible in a harsh white script.

"It is a name," Bin Starkill explained. "Mahmoud."

"MAHMOUD!" Turon Bey exclaimed excitedly and turned to his tall companion. "You know! The blind storyteller who begs alms at the new fish market they just opened at the edge of the water near the Old City. They say he is old as time itself."

Gordon Ari Bin Starkill put his hands together and began rubbing them together as a contemplative expression came over his handsome face. "Yes, yes. Of course! It has to be!"

"What?" Sinclair asked still holding her glasses out. "What has to be?"

Sinclair's question ended Bin Starkill's inner reverie and he looked at her as if seeing her for the very first time. Then he gave her a reserved smile. "If I'm right, the answer to everything, Miss Sinclair. But we've got to hurry! We've no time to waste!"

***

Twenty minutes later, after having thrown water on her face and washing up as best she could in the machine shop's loo, Nicola Sinclair had put on a clean dress and head scarf and settled herself in the back of Turon Bay's yellow Citroen. Gordon Ari Bin Starkill sat up front in the passenger seat while Bella's owner drove them to the bustling new fish market located across the road from the famous Arch of Marcus Aurelius; a popular tourist attraction.

It was mid-day and traffic was heavy as the small French taxi navigated the twisting brick covered lanes dodging bicyclists and pedestrians. As they sped past one particular outdoor café, none of them noticed the waiter wiping the top of an empty round table. But he saw them and watched as they disappeared towards the crowded piers. He threw down his dishcloth and ran back inside to the wall telephone in the rear kitchen area.

When the owner, an old woman with silver-gray hair, turned from one of the counters where pastries were made and saw him, she started to open her mouth only to have him tell her mind her own business. He hurriedly punched in a number, held the receiver to his ear and waited for someone to pick up on the other end.

"Yes?" a voice came on.

"Get the German," the waiter said. "Tell him I just saw the yellow taxi he's looking for."

***

The new modern fish market was housed in a giant building next to the docks and opened every morning at 4:30 a.m. and would remain active as long as there was stock to be sold. It was a massive, air conditioned structure equipped with three huge icemakers provided to the forty-eight vendors who sold their fresh catch from the waters of the Mediterranean in stalls lined up and divided into two long halls to serve the public.

Whereas fishermen would roll their fish laden carts into the north end of the building, visitors and would be customers would enter via the southern entrance where the main parking area was located.

As Turon Bey pulled his cab into an empty spot, Sinclair caught the pungent scent of the building's product wafting from the air-condition blowers. Climbing out of the back seat, the squall of seagulls assailed her and looking up she saw hundreds of them circling overhead.

"They are waiting for the dump carts filled with fish guts to be hauled away," Turon Bay explained. "In the meanwhile they fly around all day shitting on everything. They are the most dirty birds, Mademoiselle."

"You'll get no arguments from me," Sinclair agreed wrinkling her nose. "So where is this fellow we are looking for?"

Turon Bey pointed to the corner of the building and there they saw a cluster of tiny shacks where a group of children and a few adults were gathered around a figure seated on an old fruit crate. "That is him over there. That is Mahmoud the storyteller. Come."

They made their way past the crowds going into the giant building and joined those assembled around the blind storyteller. Mahmoud was an old man with a neatly trimmed gray beard, thick bushy eyebrows and was dressed in loose baggy pants and a cotton shirt beneath a red vest festooned with pockets. He wore a faded black turban and his face was weathered and tan. Over his eyes he wore blue-tinted glasses and across his lap he held a carved wooden stick that he used as a cane. On his feet he wore thin, orange rubber sandals.

Mahmoud's voice was of a rich, deep bass which surprised Sinclair when she heard it up close. He was just finishing a story which his audience was clearly captivated by.

"And that is how Sinbad the Sailor defeated the evil Vizier and saved the beautiful Princess Fatima."

Instantly the children in front of the storyteller began to cheer and clap their hands, delighted by the tale he had spun. Many of them had heard it many times before and loved how the old man brought it to life with his words.

"Thank you, thank you," Mahmoud picked up the tin cup that had been resting against his hip and held it out to his audience. Several adults came forth and dropped a few dinars into it. At the jingling sound, Mahmoud smiled and nodded. "The blessings of Allah on all of you this day."

Some of the children began to ask for another tale but Turon Bey rushed past them and spoke into the old man's ear quickly. Mahmoud seemed to sit up straighter and twisted his head slightly. He turned to the lad and whispered a reply. Then he addressed his audience while pulling an old pocket-watch out of his vest. Sinclair saw that the lens was missing and the blind man was able to touch its hands with his fingertips thus allowing to him to tell his listeners that it was time for his afternoon lunch and that he would come back to the market later that evening; weather permitting.

As the children reluctantly went off with their parents, Sinclair and Bin Starlin came forward. Turon Bey was helping the old storyteller off his perch. With his feet solidly only the ground, Mahmoud held his four foot cane with his left hand and faced them.

"My friends, this is Mahmoud," Turon Bey made the introductions. "Old one, this is Gordon Ari Bin Starkill and Mademoiselle Nicola Sinclair."

"The priest and the spy," the blind man said and bowed slightly. "Salaam to you both."

"Salaam," Bin Starkill returned confused. "But I am no priest, old one."

"Bah," Mahmoud shrugged. "What's in a title is never as important as what is in one's heart. But come, let us go inside where we can speak in private." He indicated the small shack behind them.

"Very well," Bin Starkill pulled Turon Bey aside. "Stay out here and keep watch. If El Shaira is still looking for Nicola, we have to stay on guard."

"Understood; I'll wander through the fish market and keep my eyes open. Maybe I'll buy us some fresh fish for dinner." The boy playfully swatted Bin Starkill on the arm and started back through the parking grounds merrily whistling as he did so.

"After you, old one," Bin Starkill told Mahmoud. The blind man, using his cane, made his way to the shack's single door and opened it. He walked inside followed by Sinclair and Bin Starkill.

It was a tiny two-room abode, with the bedroom and toilet off to the right as they entered. The main room consisted of a living area with a single couch and several chairs. Against the back wall, where a single window looked out towards the harbor and sea, there was a sink, gas stove and a dented icebox set on the counter to the right of the sink.

Once in the room, Mahmoud easily navigated around the two padded chairs and went to sit on the old couch which was covered by a knitted blue blanket. Behind the couch was a single bookshelf filled with religious bric-a-brac from a Buddhist prayer bead to a statue of St. Francis and a bronze Star of David.

Nicola Sinclair, as was her occupational habit, unconsciously surveyed the tiny dwelling, her eyes picking up minute details. The only in or out was the front door, though there was another window in the bedroom through which one could exit if another means of departure were required.

"If you are thirsty, I've sweet tea in the icebox," Mahmoud offered as he sat back. He pointed to the appliance with his cane. Both politely declined. "Then please, sit and make yourselves comfortable." This time the stick was aimed at the two chairs side by side facing him.

"So why did you call me a spy?" Sinclair asked after sitting.

Before answering her, Mahmoud reached into another of his vest pockets and found a disposable lighter which he threw in Bin Starkill's direction. The tall brown man, who was just about to seat himself, reacted swiftly and caught the lighter easily. Hearing it smack into his palm, the blind man grinned and pointed down to the hookah bowl on the floor to left of the sofa. "If you would be so kind as to light my pipe?"

Bin Starkill chuckled and gladly obliged their host. Before getting off his knees, he handed the blind man back his lighter and the stemmed mouthpiece affixed to glass bowl. The waterpipe made a gurgling sound as its flavored tobacco (*shisha)* began to vaporize sending a thin line of smoke rising from its plastic tip. Mahmoud took it in his mouth, inhaled and then blew out an aromatic cloud that smelled of fresh cut cinnamon.

"Thank you," Mahmound as he smoked contentedly. "I called you a spy, young lady, because our mutual friend, Mr. Porter told me if he did not return from the desert, you might be the one sent to find him."

"Wait a minute," Sinclair leaned forward. "You knew Porter too?" Bin Starkill shook his head indicating he was personally unaware of that particular fact.

"Yes, my dear. You see, I'm the one who told him where to find the Tree of Life even though I warned him to seek it out might cost him his life."

"You know where it is?" Bin Starkill queried before Sinclair could say anything further. The look on his face was one of true surprise.

"But of course, young man." Mahmoud took the pipe stem from his mouth and tapped his chest with it. "You see, I am the Guardian. It is my task to see to its protection and safety. A holy task I have not shirked for two hundred years."

At that last claim both Sinclair and Bin Starkill looked at each other in disbelief.

Sinclair slapped the arm of her chair. "Enough. Please. This is all going a bit too fast for me, gentlemen. Before I can even learn what this is all about, now I'm asked to believe I'm dealing with someone who is two hundred years old. I'm sorry, but would both of you kindly take a moment and start from the beginning."

"She does not know about the Tree?" Mahmoud directed his question to Bin Starkill.

"Ah, no…I was hoping if we found Alan Porter's guide…and it now appears we have…that he…you, Mahmoud would be so kind as to do so."

Mahmoud sat back and relaxed his shoulders, his blind eyes seeming to be staring into space. Then he sighed. "Yes, I suppose that does make sense.

"Miss Sinclair, are you familiar with the Creation Myth?"

"You mean from the bible?"

"Yes, more directly, as set down in the Jewish holy books, the Torah. The story of creation is told in the *Bereshit,* which is Hebrew for Genesis."

"Well, yes. We were taught the tale of how God made the world in seven days and then populated it with the animals and fauna. On the last day he made Adam and Eve and that's how mankind began."

"Very good," Mahmoud smiled. "Do you recall where Yahweh, God set them in this wonderful fairy tale?"

"It was the Garden of Eden."

"Correct. And what happened to Adam and Even in this paradise on Earth?"

Niki Sinclair crossed one leg over the other and wondered where the old man was going with his impromptu testing of her. "Well, yes. God said they could eat from all the trees and plants in the garden except one; a certain apple tree from which they were forbidden to eat."

"Excellent, young lady. And do you remember what was so important about this tree that made it so special?"

"Yes, I do. The tree supposedly contained all wisdom to include the knowledge of what was good and what was evil. This was knowledge God was unwilling to share with them. Then the Devil, a fallen angel from heaven, came to Eve disguised as a snake and convinced her to disobey God. He told her that if they ate from this tree, they would be as wise and all knowing as God. So she was tempted and did as the snake told her. The second Adam and Eve ate the apple, they both understood good and evil and thus the fact that they had disobeyed God. For this transgression, they were expelled from the Garden of Eden and made to suffer all of this world's trials and tribulations….including death."

"Wonderful," Mahmoud clapping his rough hands together. "You could be a storyteller yourself, Miss Sinclair."

"Thank you, but what does that mean? Are you saying this tree of good and evil is this so-called Tree of Life everyone is obsessed with?"

"Not quite. You see, the story you just related is the one most people, of all religions, know in one form or another. Very few people, other than scholars and priests, pay attention to the complete story. You see, Miss Sinclair, the Book of Genesis actually tells of two trees. The one you just now described, the one we call the Tree of Knowledge. But in the ancient Greek scrolls the story also tells of a second tree: the Tree of Life. A tree whose fruit would grant the partaker eternal life....free of death. Simply put who ever eats from this tree will never die."

"And you say that's in the bible."

"Most assuredly. You see, the Creator intended man to share eternity with him, thus he was created to live forever. But before the Creator would grant him that blessing, he had to be sure man was not tainted with evil.... or else evil would also become eternal."

"So the Tree of Knowledge was really a test?" Sinclair saw the pieces falling into place. Considering her lack of any formalized religious education, she was amazed she remembered as much as she had. Maybe there were more to these myths than people believed.

"Indeed, my dear lady," Mahmoud went on. "Had Adam and Eve not fallen to the serpent's temptation and corrupted themselves with the knowledge of good and evil, the Creator would have given them the fruit from the Tree of Life and made them immortal. But when they sinned, they were cast out, forever forbidden to partake of this miraculous Tree of Life."

"And that is what this is all about. El Shaira is looking for this Tree of Life?'

"Yes."

"Because he believes it actually exists and if it eats from it, he'll become immortal."

"Again, yes."

Nicola Sinclair uncrossed her legs and took a long breath. Words escaped her.

"You are skeptical, Miss Sinclair?" Mahmoud teased.

"Skeptical! But of course I am. You can't seriously expect me to believe that this Tree of Life actually exists...out there, somewhere in the middle of the desert."

"You may not wish to believe. That is your prerogative, young lady. But you are mistaken."

"So you are telling me this tree is real. That it's out there, lost somewhere."

"Oh, it is not lost, Miss Sinclair. I know exactly where it is. Which is why Alan Porter came to me…and no doubt why this Mr. El Shaira is also looking for me. You see, as I said earlier, I am the tree's Holy Guardian."

Mahmoud put down his pipe stem and carefully unwound the turban off his nearly bald head. Still smiling at his guests, he ran a hand over his round head slick with sweat.

Bin Starkill was having trouble comprehending the old blind man's revelations. "So you told Alan where to find the Tree because he simply asked you where it was to be found?"

"Of course. It is my duty to answer all such inquiries honestly. It is not my charge to stop anyone from finding the Tree. But I do have a responsibility to warn them of the dangers should they pursue such a journey."

"Dangers such as what?" The Taureg wasn't as put off as the lovely British agent. He had seen too many strange and wondrous things while growing up in the Sahara. Things man's science could never properly explain. If Mahmoud was telling them the truth, then it behooved them to learn everything they could.

"There is a sand creature known as the Katari," Mahmoud said. "It was made solely to keep men from the Tree."

"I have never of such a thing."

Mahmoud chuckled. "That is because they only exist near the Tree. Imagine a scorpion the size of a dog….only with two tails. That is a Katari and they will attack any who seek the Tree's sacred fruit."

The old man's story was getting crazier by the minute, Sinclair thought to herself. *A magic tree in the desert that bestows eternal life and now giant scorpions to defend it. No wonder people loved this fellow's storytelling. He was certainly a master at spinning tall tales.*

Just then the front door banged open and Turon Bey came charging in. He directed his words to Bin Starkill. "El Shaira's Berbers! They're here!" He pointed past the open door to the large parking area. "There're several jeeps and pick-up trucks filled with them!"

"We have to go!" Bin Starkill jumped to his feet as did Sinclair.

"But I have not told you the location of the Tree of Life?" Mahmoud pushed off the sofa.

"That will have to wait," Sinclair said, drawing her Peashooter from a pocket in her skirt. "If we survive the next few minutes, we'll return. Thank you for your help." She turned and started after Turon Bay who was already half out the door.

"Wait!" Mahmoud reached out with his cane and hit Bin Starkill's arm as he was starting to follow Sinclair.

"Yes, old one?"

"If you go after the Tree, leave your guns behind, priest. They will not work in that place. It is holy ground. Remember that."

"I will, Allah bless you a hundredfold, old one." Then Gordon Ari Bin Starkill fled out the door after his friends leaving the blind man alone.

***

Once outside, Sinclair spotted the vehicles Turon Bey had described. She could see the convoy of two jeeps and two pick-up trucks just coming off the main boulevard and into the tightly packed parking square. Each of the pick-up trucks carried a half dozen Berbers, all carrying various automatic weapons; most were Russian made AK-47s with banana clips.

The innocent citizens, upon seeing the armed warriors, all began to flee in whatever direction was open to them; weaving their way around the parked automobiles.

Sinclair cautioned Turon Bey to get down in a crouch as they began to hustle towards his yellow Citroen at the opposite end of the lot. Bin Starkill raced up behind them and also dropped down while pulling a .45 Colt automatic from a shoulder rig hidden under his shirt.

They were almost at Turon's small sedan when the driver of the lead jeep spotted them running through an open area and began shouting to his companions. The Berbers standing in the open back of the jeep immediately began firing with their machine guns sending a spray of deadly bullets randomly through the parking grounds. A middle-aged fish merchant was hit in the back and fell with a piercing cry. Frantically, some of his friends dragged him to safety behind the nearest parked truck.

Nicola Sinclair could not believe the cruel, insensitivity of these killers to open fire in such a public place. She had no doubts more people would be injured unless she and her companions could reach their car and get away from there. Failing that, the fish market yard would quickly become the setting for a bloody massacre, especially after the police arrived and joined the battle. Most likely they would end up shooting at anything that moved.

As the enemy vehicles continued to make their way through the narrow lanes, the Berbers continued shooting at the fleeing trio. As bullets spanged off the tops of cars behind which they hid, Sinclair's patience expired and, without a thought to her own safety, she stood up, aimed her small-but-powerful Peashooter and pulled the trigger.

The front jeep's windshield shattered as the bullet went through it and whacked the driver between the eyes. Blood and gore ripped from the back of his head as he slumped forward dead. The wheel in his lifeless hands spun to the left and the jeep plowed into a parked mini-van knocking the two men in the back over the front seat. They crashed head first onto the engine hood and then fell senseless to the hard tarmac.

Then Sinclair and her allies were at the Citroen and quickly climbed into it. Turon Bey got the engine going, shoved the shift into reverse and backed out of the space. Bullets careened off the trunk as he shoved the stick into first, popped the clutch and sent the yellow car speeding forward.

"Get us out of this place," Bin Starkill shouted as he pointed to the alleyway that ran alongside the main building. "There. It leads to the wharfs and piers!"

Turon screamed at pedestrians to get out of his way and barely missed a young woman with a baby in her arms. He turned out of the parking lot and into the shadowy alleyway. Behind them the second jeep along with the two pick-up trucks was in hot pursuit. They were almost at the end of the passage when bullets smashed into the rear window sending millions of shards of glass raining into the interior.

Sinclair, in the backseat, cried out, and ducked down while throwing her arms up over the back of her head. Tiny pieces of glass cut into her bare arms like needle pricks.

"Bollocks!" she cursed feeling the air whip over her and out the open slot where the window had been. Angrily she sat up, carefully turned around on the debris covered seat and fired two quick shots out the opening at the on-rushing jeep. The first slug hit the jeep's engine grill while the second caught the man in the passenger seat in the chest causing him to throw his hands up into the air and toppled out of the racing jeep. Three seconds later the first pick-up truck ran over his body.

Coming out of the alley, Turon Bey jerked the wheel hard to the left and the Citroen dance around the corner on two wheels for several yards before falling back onto all four.

The wharf was a nightmare of stacked pallets, crates and moving fork-lifts. Frantically Turon pulled the steering wheel back and forth while at the same time hitting his horn to alert dock-workers and fishermen to get out of his way. The car hit several uneven wooden slats causing it to bounce up and down, its riders hitting the steel roof with their heads.

"Bloody hell, Turon!" Sinclair yelled wishing the boy could have at least put seat belts in the damn car. "Try not to get us killed before those Berbers do the job!"

"Sorry, Mademoiselle," the anxious lad retorted, keeping his grip on the wheel. "I assure you, I am doing my best."

Ahead of them to the right were towering cranes in the process of lifting giant pallets of cargo and deftly maneuvering them over the docks to drop them in their designated area. Turon Bey did his best to ignore them as he kept his focus on the many sailors and stevedores in front of them. His palm kept slapping the horn and men kept scrambling out of his way; some at the last minute.

They were nearing a long pier that jutted out between two anchored tankers. The lad gave it no heed but rather twisted the wheel to avoid a stack of steel cargo containers to his left. As he was straightening out the wheel, a lone figure emerged from behind these containers to stand directly in their path.

It was Gunther Friedoff and in his hands he held a AK-47.

"Look out!" Bin Starkill warned too late, as the big German mercenary, dressed in a khaki uniform and baseball cap, raised the weapon's stock into his shoulder and let loose a barrage of hot lead. The bullets exploded the front windshield and it seemed to vanish in the blink of an eye, while the deadly missiles tore into Turon Bay riddling his chest and neck. Blood gushed from his mouth as he tried to keep control of the car.

In the back seat, Sinclair had fallen to the floor. One bullet had ripped at her hair as she fell. In the passenger seat, Bin Starkill had been grazed along the side of the head but in the heat of the moment wasn't aware of the wound. Rather he leaned over and wrenched the wheel towards him… and out of the dying boy's hands.

The Citroen cut right and rocketed onto the long pier causing workers to dive out of the way. Blood seeped into Bin Starkill's eyes as the small car raced over the wooden planks towards the end of the pier. Behind them, Friedoff had continued firing at them, his salvo tearing into the trunk with loud thunking sounds.

"SINCLAIR!" Bin Starkill cried out as the yellow car drove towards the end of the dock.

She lifted herself up behind him and saw Turon Bay slumped against his door, his eyes glazed seeing nothing, his blood smeared mouth gaping wide. Something inside her cried. Then she looked past Bin Starkill as he let go of the wheel and brought his hands up to cover his face.

The car plunged off the pier, its front end flipping over so that it hit the water on its roof where it made a big splash. Then water flooded in from all its broken windows and Turon Bey's beloved Bella sank into the deep dark waters of the Mediterranean.

***

"Get in there," Gunther Friedoff snapped as he pushed blind Mahmoud into Arman El Shaira's command tent. El Shaira was seated behind his folding tent drinking coffee and working on his laptop computer. He looked up when he heard them enter unannounced. He saw his chief lieutenant pulling the old man by the scruff of his shirt so that he almost fell over. Only his cane kept him upright.

"What's this all about?" El Shaira closed his laptop and glared at Friedoff annoyed at having been interrupted.

"The A.C.T.I.O.N. agent, Herr Shaira, we found her and her comrades."

"Where?"

"The new fish market on the docks. They attempted to flee and their automobile fell into the harbor. They all drowned."

"You are positive?"

"I watched for twenty minutes before we heard the police coming. They were all shot to pieces before their car plunged into the water. You have my word, none of them survived."

El Shaira put his hands together and touched his chin with the tips of his fingers. "Good. That is one less headache I have to contend with. Maybe now A.C.T.I.O.N. will think twice before interfering with my plans."

Then the rich oil tycoon turned his gaze to the bareheaded old man next to his top soldier. "Who is this fellow and why have you brought him to me?"

Hearing the question, Mahmoud stood straight and turned to El Shaira. "I am Mahmoud, the storyteller."

"The female spy had gone to the area to seek this one out," Friedoff added. "I thought if he was so important to her, you might want to see him."

"Really?" El Shaira was intrigued and gave the little man closer scrutiny. "Is it true, old one? Did the British agent seek you out?"

Before the blind man could answer, Professor Anlo Pareen poked his head inside the tent. "Excuse me, El Shaira, could I have a word with you?"

"Can't you see I'm busy? Oh, very well. Come in…but make it quick."

Pareen entered carrying several ancient scrolls and hurried to El Shaira's table. As he walked around the old man with the tinted glasses, he saw the cane in Mahmoud's hand.

"We've translated more of the Greek maps," the noted archeologist began but his gaze kept going back to the polished wooden stick. He clumsily handed the scrolls to El Shaira almost knocking over the cup of coffee.

"What?" El Shaira saw his chief archeologist was distracted.

"Ah…excuse me," Prof. Pareen nervously rubbed his hands together and turned towards Mahmoud. "May I inquire as to this gentlemen's identity?"

"He is supposedly a storyteller who earlier this afternoon met with the British agent sent to uncover our mission. His name is Mahmoud. Why?"

"Ah…I'm not sure….but I sense something about him." Pareen took a step closer to the blind man and pointed down at his cane. "May I see your cane?"

Mahmoud turned his head to the scientist and smiled. "That's more than I can do, scholar." He handed Pareen his cane.

"Ow!" Upon touching it, Pareen had felt a mild electric shock. Holding it firmly, he brought it up close to his eyes where a word had been carved into the length of stick. He held it out towards El Shaira. "Look, see that word etched on it?"

"Yes. What is it?"

"It's Hebrew for life." The professor was clearly excited and returned his attention to Mahmoud. "Tell me, where did you get this cane?"

Mahmoud smiled and said, "I cut it from the Tree of Life."

El Shaira jumped to his feet. Could the answer they had been searching for all these months actually be standing only a few feet in front of him in the shape of this old blind Arab.

"I believe," Prof. Pareen said confirming his employer's supposition, "we've found our guide."

***

It was sunset and a blazing sky slid into the western horizon beyond the tall minarets of Tripoli. Nicola Sinclair came tumbling out of the three foot waves that lapped against the tiny beach two miles south of the harbor. With her left hand she clung to Gordon Ari Bin Starkill's collar pulling him along after her. As his body washed onto the hard pebble beach, she began coughing up salt water; emptying her tired lungs that gasped for air. With her last ounce of strength she dragged the unconscious Bin Starkill out of the surf along side her.

Then she took hold of his arm and shoulder and turned him over onto his face and stomach. Much to her agonized relief he was still breathing despite the nasty cut along his temple just above his left ear. That was where the bullet had grazed him just before they went into the drink.

Exhausted, Sinclair fell over onto her back and looked up at the darkling sky. Blue was morphing into purple and soon night would descend completely. She laid her head back and closed her eyes while continuing to breathe deeply.

Images spun around in her mind like a crazy carousel and she could see herself in the sinking Citroen as it rapidly sank into the black depths of the harbor. The water had flooded the car's interior so fast she'd barely had time to take in a lungful of air and hold it in. Completely inundated, she'd opened her eyes and in the rapidly fading light held onto the front seat to examine how her two friends had fared. The gush of blood surrounding Turon Bey's head told her he was dead. She tugged at Bin Starkill's shoulder and saw air bubbles escaping his open mouth. He was still alive.

She managed to get her hands under his arms and bracing her feet against the floorboards, pull him up and back. With the auto descending deeper and deeper with each passing second, she knew their time was running out fast. Thus as he came up out of the front seat, Sinclair brought her feet up against its back and shoved for all she was worth. She went up through the open back window and out of the sinking vehicle with Bin Starkill in her hands. Free of the car she began kicking with her feet and slowly they began to rise to the surface.

In the dim light she could see the bottom of the pier and knew surfacing next to it in open water would put them in immediate jeopardy. The big man with the machine-gun had to be waiting up there to make sure they were finished. So she twisted her body around and directed them away from that particular pier and towards the main docks.

Finally, after what felt like an eternity, her head came out of the water and she coughed spitting out salt water from her mouth. Grabbing onto one of the huge round pylons, she pulled Bin Starkill's head out of the water and feebly tried to shake his shoulders. With one hand on the pylon,

Sinclair brought her legs up and wrapped them around the comatose man's middle. Once secured, she used her free hand to slap him hard in the back between his shoulder blades. When that elicited no response she did it again…and again.

"Come on you bastard, breathe!" she cursed.

A fourth slap did the trick and Bin Starkill's head jerked and his mouth opened to spew out water. He coughed and then looking at her, his eyes rolled in their socket and he passed out again.

Great! But at least he was alive.

The water below the docks was cold with clumps of seaweed floating all around them. Sinclair guessed that if she could follow the docks and swim to the south they would eventually reach open water and safety. At least that was her hope.

With grim determination, she released her legs from around the sleeping Bin Starkill and wrapped her left arm about his neck. Then, as she'd been taught in Red Cross swimming classes as a teen, Nicola Sinclair began swimming with her precious cargo in tow.

That had been over an hour ago and now she could only look up at the twinkling stars as they heralded the coming of night. Thoughts of a smiling, laughing Turon Bey overwhelmed her and tears rolled down her already wet cheeks. Their clothing was soaked, their weapons were gone and they were stretched out on a vulnerable beach.

There was a motion beside her followed by a cough and intake of breath.

"Where are we?" Bin Starkill was awake.

"Away from the docks," she replied. "Safe for the time being."

Silence followed and then, "I remember now. It was the German, Friedoff." Another pause. "Turon Bey?"

"He didn't make it, Ari. He was dead before we hit the water."

"But…how…you…you pulled us out?"

"Affirmative. It was close for a while, but we made it."

"I owe you my life, Nicola."

"You'll have plenty of chances to settle the score later. Right now we need to get out of here. Wherever here is and get back to your place."

"Yes, of course. You'll want to report back to your people." Bin Starkill climbed to his feet, steadied himself and then offered her his hand. Sinclair grabbed hold of it and got to her feet. Beyond them they could see a road, street lamps and speeding traffic.

"Know where we are?"

"I've an idea. It shouldn't take us long to get to the machine shop from here."

"Good, because after I report back to A.C.T.I.O.N. there's something we have to do."

He put his arms about her waist and holding onto her they began to walk off the beach and towards the street. "What's that, Lady Action?"

"I'm going to find this Gunther Friedoff and kill him."

"Good, because if you don't, I will."

***

The A.C.T.I.O.N. Commander woke every day at 4:30 in the morning. Ten minutes later, dressed in a blue jogging outfit and matching baseball cap, she was out on the road for her morning ten mile jog. The run would take her through the still sleeping town of Sleaford and through several cabbage farms before making a loop and bringing her back to A.C.T.I.O.N. Headquarters.

On this particular morning, a light pre-dawn rain fell but she didn't mind it at all. The rain felt good against her face as she ran easily over the mostly dirt roads. Her legs ate up the ground and with the endurance of her special artificial limb, she easily maintained her pace for hours. Unfortunately the pleasant solitude of these morning runs was always fleeting and even as the first rays of a lightening sky appeared behind her she could see someone awaiting her at the building's main entrance.

She recognized Night Shift Director, Ed Catto. He was holding a towel for her.

"You've an incoming communiqué from field agent Lady Action."

"How long has it been on hold?" She took the towel and wiped her face, then removed her cap and began to towel her hair. All the while she was marching through the lobby with Catto hurrying behind her.

"Only five minutes now," he stated glancing at his wristwatch.

"Thank, you, Ed. I'll take it in my office."

Eight minutes later the Commander entered her private office, switched on the lights and then sat behind her desk where her computer screen was lit with the A.C.T.I.O.N. logo.

"Activate," she spoke and the face of Nicola Sinclair appeared. The Commander saw she was dressed in a Bedouin robe (abaya) while seated in what appeared to be a machine shop and looked anxious but alert. "Lady Action, good to see you are still in one piece."

"Thank you, Sir," her daughter said stoically.

"Have you found Agent Porter?"

"No, Sir, but his whereabouts are known."

"Fine. Proceed with your report, Lady Action."

For the next ten minutes, Nicola Sinclair reported her findings since arriving in Tripoli from being picked up by Turon Bey to her breaking into Porter's apartment, meeting Gordon Ari Bin Starkill, the introduction to Mahmoud and her narrow escape from death at the hands of Arman El Shaira's mercenaries.

When she was finished, she took a breath and waited for her Commander's reaction.

"Interesting indeed," the former model commented. "I've heard some fairly wild stories in my life but this one ranks with the wildest yet. Tell me, Lady Action, what do you make of it? Do you believe this old man and his legend about a magical tree from the Garden of Eden?"

"I really can't say, Commander. All I do know is that El Shaira believes it. Enough to kill over it and assure no one else finds it before him."

"And you think that was Agent Porter's fate?"

"Everything points to that conclusion, Sir."

"Yes, it does, doesn't it." The Commander bit down on her lower lip, a gesture Nicola Sinclair had seen many times in her life. Her mother's calculating mind was at work. "Very well then, do you think El Shaira is going to go after the Tree now?"

"If he has Mahmoud, that would be my guess, Sir."

"Then you will follow him..."

Sinclair started to speak but the Commander held up her index finger. "I said follow! Do I make my self clear, Lady Action?"

"Yes, Commander."

"Under no circumstances are you to engage El Shaira's forces. The odds are against you and it would be suicide. If he should find this Tree of Life, as you call it, then you will contact HQ with the coordinates and a Strike Force will be dispatched."

"Understood Commander." Sinclair began to switch off the connection. The Commander leaned in closer and looked her directly in the eyes.

"Be careful, dear."

The monitor went black.

***

Nicola Sinclair heard Bin Starkill's BSA motorcycle through the back door as it came to a quick stop. She was closing her laptop when he came into the room carrying a brown canvas duffel bag and looking agitated.

"They're gone!" he dumped the heavy bag on the table careful not to hit her laptop or shake the pot of coffee from which she'd been drinking.

"Who? El Shaira and his people?" She took one last swallow of the robust brew in her cup and then pushed her chair away from the table to stand.

"Yes, their entire campsite is deserted. The people I had watching it told me they packed everything up in the middle of the night and rolled out just before dawn heading due south."

"So El Shaira has obviously learned something about the Tree's location."

"No, it's even worse," Bin Starkill corrected. "My spies report seeing an old blind man being shoved into one of the fancy desert vehicles. He was carrying a cane and being guarded carefully by a big soldier."

"Mahmoud! It has to be! Friedoff must have picked him up after he thought we were finished."

"Yes, and the old man will lead them directly to the Tree. He as much as told us so."

"Then we don't have a minute to spare, Ari. We have to go after them."

"Yes, Lady Action. Which is why I retrieved these arms for us." The tall Taureg agent of the Church unzipped the duffel bag and pulled it open. Inside were dozens of small hand guns, knives and swords.

From the cache, Bin Starkill pulled out a three foot long Arab scimitar and ran a thumb along its razor-liked edge.

"Are we going native here?" Sinclair nodded at the blade in his hand.

Bin Starkill found the scabbard for the sword in the bag and smoothly sheathed the beautiful weapon. "Before leaving his shack, Mahmoud warned me that modern firearms would prove useless where the Tree is located. Something to do with whatever arcane magic surrounds it. Ergo, I thought it wise to bring along these more reliable tools that my ancestors fought with."

Sinclair smiled and went to find her suitcase still resting atop the sleeping cot. She bent down and taking the aluminum carrying case, turned it over onto its side. Then her fingers touched a tiny slot at the base of the suitcase and a thin plate sprung open. Digging her fingers into the hideaway slot, she used them to dig out a long two and a half foot sword designed with three serrated edges.

Bin Starkill had come closer and whistled when he saw what she was holding.

"I've never seen a sword shaped like that?" he admitted.

"It's standard A.C.T.I.O.N. issue and the steel is forged with a special alloy that was mined from a meteorite making it virtually unbreakable."

"But what about a hilt?" He was pointing the tip at the other non-lethal end of the unique weapon.

"It's right here," Sinclair said as she turned her attention to the suitcase's handle. She deftly twisted it free and then found a tiny button that opened the grip like a butterfly spreading its wings. The naked hilt of her sword fitted into this detached handle and she snapped it shut over the steel. Standing, she hefted it and did a few quick strokes showing her friend she was no novice to its proper handling.

"All right, I'm impressed," Bin Starkill grinned. "Lets see what else we want to load up with and then after I've changed into my desert togs, we can get moving."

"But how? Did you get us a Land Rover or some such. I mean, we won't get far in the desert on your motorbike."

"Oh, have no worries about our transportation, Lady Action. I've already seen to that and they are even now being prepared for us."

"They?"

"Yes. I've bought us three camels."

***

Arman El Shaira's motorized caravan made its way over the golden sands of the Deep Desert like a giant, disjointed metal worm. Since leaving Tripoli, the expedition had covered thirty-five miles in its journey heading southeast. El Shaira sat in the rear of the second of four half-track vehicles with the heavy rubber tank-threads that spit up sand as they rolled along. Behind these were two Land Rovers and three American Jeeps. Riding with the wealthy Arab were Prof. Arlo Pareen and several of the Yugoslavian's academic colleagues. In the front seat were two of Gunther Friedoff's Berber mercenaries, one driver and the other a guard. Friedoff himself, was in the lead vehicle with their reluctant guide, Mahmoud.

"It is still difficult for me to wrap my head around all this," the suave playboy billionaire admitted to the wise archeologist. "How is it possible? What that old man does?"

"You mean with his cane?" Prof. Pareen looked from his iPad where he had been looking over topographical maps.

"Yes. He simply holds it up before him and then tells us to go whichever way it points. It reminds me of those stories about people who could find water using a divining rod."

"That's a good analogy, though I suspect the fact that the cane itself was hewn from the Tree is the reason for its being able to point to its location."

"I'm surprised, Pareen, a man of science like yourself accepting so outlandish a proposition. Doesn't it go against everything you believe?"

"My dear, El Shaira, in my life I've encountered many things I could not explain. But that does not infer that I give any credence to magic. No, far from it. But at the same time, I am willing to admit there remain many mysteries in this world and as a scientist it is my duty to study these phenomena.

"Whatever it is that old man is doing is simply beyond our current understanding. But in time, if given the opportunity to examine these so-called abilities clinically, a rational scientific explanation will be discovered."

El Shaira took a silk handkerchief from his shirt pocket and removing his sunglasses, began to wipe the lenses clean. "And the Tree of Life? Is that also something you think can be explained by your radium carbon machines and test tubes?"

Pareen shrugged. "I'll address that mystery when…and if…we find it."

"Oh, we are going to find it, Professor," El Shaira eased his sunglasses back on looking out at the desolate land they traversed. "It is my destiny to find it. Of that I am certain."

The caravan continued on its way over small and large dunes going deeper and deeper into the no-man's land where a new mile looked exactly like the one before it. All the while the burning red ball in the sky above continued to beat down on them.

By late afternoon they spotted a dozen palm trees at the bottom of a ravine and knew they had reached the Oasis of Sal Arum. At its center was a deep water well used by Bedouin traders when crossing this part of the desert. It was the last such oasis to be found on any maps. Beyond it lay the vast unknown.

Friedoff's experienced Berbers suggested they make camp for the night and El Shaira concurred. The vehicles formed a wide circle around the oasis and soon tents were being erected as others set about making a campfire.

***

Far behind El Shaira's camp, three ungainly Dromedary camels plodded over the desert as the sky over head began to darken. Nicola Sinclair, dressed from head to toe in Bedouin robes, face and head scarves, hung on to the pommel of her soft leather saddle as her camel trod along, its every step pure torture on her derriere.

"I don't think my spine is ever going to be straight again," she complained to Gordon Ari Bin Starkill who rode along beside her on his own four-legged mount. Unlike her, he had ridden the six foot single humped beasts often and learned to keep his body loose as the creature marched along.

"You're fighting it," he told her. "I told you, there is no easy way to ride a camel. They don't have an even gait like a horse."

"Tell me something I don't know," Sinclair groused. "I'm never going to get used to this up and down, side to side jostling."

"Ha, ha. Trust me, yes you will. You just have to relax your body, Nicola. Once you do that, it will simply adjust to your animal's natural rhythm."

"Rhythm! You have got to be kidding me!" The camel took a short step and she was shoved to the side. "Aagh. Damn stupid bastard!"

Bin Starkill had everything he could do not laugh again. Dressed in the royal blue of his people, the Taureg felt at home here in this dry wilderness atop his camel with its thick coat of tan colored hair. A rope tied to his pommel pulled along their third camel which carried their provisions.

"Why didn't we just get a Land Rover to go after El Shaira? Wouldn't that have been easier....and faster?" The only thing visible of the A.C.T.I.O.N. agent were the lenses of her Raybans between the folds of her face scarf. Bin Starkill imagined they were piercing him like daggers.

"Perhaps," he conceded. "But try to understand this. In all the world, there is no greater desert than the one we are entering. Even in this modern age of wondrous technology, the Libyan Deep Desert is considered an uncharted region whose temperatures can easily exceed 70 degrees Celsius. The deeper we go, it will be as if we were walking onto a natural frying pan."

"Okay, I get it, Ari. It's going to be hot. And your point is?"

"One of the things we Taureg learned ages ago, other than the human body, nothing long endures in the desert; including fancy driving machines. Our best chance of succeeding is in adapting the old ways of the desert people."

They rode along in silence for the next few minutes as Sinclair thought over her friend's logic. When she spoke, it was with a touch of sarcasm. "I hope you are right about that, Ari, because if I ended up crippled and lame after this, I am never going to forgive you."

Bin Starkill couldn't help but laugh as he nodded to Lady Action. "Very well, I have justifiably been warned."

"And I'm going to shoot this thing," she finished, pointing to her camel's knobby triangular head, "right between its beady little eyes."

***

After the sun had set, Bin Starkill led them into a shallow wadi where they made camp for the night. Sinclair had brought her smartphone with its portable battery that ran on solar power. Bin Starkill had left the absorbing plate affixed to one of the carry bags on the load-camel's back thus it was able to keep the battery charged to full capacity.

Bin Starkill made a small fire with small pieces of kindling and dozens of camel ball droppings. He explained that the animal's internal water preserving belly was so efficient, its waste was always dry as old leaves and burned easily though with a rather pungent odor.

As they warmed themselves by the flames, Sinclair contacted A.C.T.I.O.N. Headquarters using her earbud. She was happy upon hearing Byron Fitzwalter's voice come through loud and clear. He informed her that A.C.T.I.O.N. was following El Shaira's motorcade via satellite imagery and that they were at the moment to be found stationary at the Oasis of Sal Arum.

"I've got a question for you, love?" Her controller asked from half-way around the world.

"What?'

"Do you have some kind of tracking device planted on one of their vehicles?'

Sinclair looked across the snapping fire at Bin Starkill who was chewing on an energy bar. "No, why?"

"Because, dear Lady Action, we're picking up a transmitting signal from them. The kind put out by a tracking bug."

I ....wait a second." She signaled the Taureg with her hand and he put down his half eaten oats and honey treat. "My controller says there is a tracking bug on one of El Shaira's vehicles."

"I know. One of my people put it there a few days ago. It was added insurance if they should depart before we were ready to follow. I was afraid we might lose sight of their tire tracks and wanted another way to track them. I have the receiver in our bags somewhere."

"And you what? Simply forgot to tell me."

"I'm sorry, but yes. What with all that was happening, it just skipped my mind. Please forgive me. I take it the bug is working after all."

"Yes, my controller said they are picking up loud and clear."

"Good. Let's hope it keeps working."

Bin Starkill took a sip from a waterskin, a pouch made from a goat-bladder, and went back to finishing his simple meal while Sinclair explained to Fitzwalter what he'd told her.

"Your mate seems competent enough."

"Oh, yes. I couldn't have gotten this far without him."

"Good. We'll expect you to maintain this routine and expect your next contact at this hour tomorrow."

"Affirmative. Lady Action out."

Upon hearing her end her private telecommunication report, Bin Starkill tossed her an energy bar. "Eat and then let's get some sleep. If they are at Sal Arum, we have a long ways to go to keep up with them."

Nicola Sinclair began unwrapping the energy food while tugging the heavy blanket she was wrapped in. Looking up she marveled at the millions of stars and wondered if life on any of those other worlds was a complicated and dangerous and those on Earth.

Time would tell.

***

For the next three days, Nicola Sinclair and Gordon Ari Bin Starkill followed El Shaira's convoy as it traveled further into the heart of the Deep Desert. On the afternoon of the second day they came upon three abandoned vehicles, two Land Rovers buried in the sand up to their wheel mounts and a short distance later a Jeep flipped over onto its back at the bottom of steep dune. Under the Jeep were two dead men who had been crushed to death in the fall. Sinclair began to understand Bin Starkill's wariness at the fragility of modern transportation in such an inhospitable terrain.

Later that night, while in the middle of her session with A.C.T.I.O.N. Headquarters, Byron's voice was suddenly drowned out in a wave of loud, steady crackling static. And then it went completely dead. When she told Bin Starkill, he went to their load-carrying camel and checked his portable radio receiver; the one they had used to tack the convoy. When he switched it on, nothing happened. Like the Sinclair's smart-phone and battery pack, it too was no longer functioning.

He shoved it back into the camel's pack and said, "That's it, Lady Action. From now on we are on our own and at the mercy of the desert."

They were grim words that echoed in her thoughts when she fell asleep that night.

❋❋❋

The next day Niki Sinclair and Bin Starkill traveled in silence. Both of them could sense a change in the atmosphere as they road over an eerie flat plain devoid of even the slightest gust of wind. By late afternoon, Sinclair noticed the wispy cumulus clouds had vanished and the sky above took on the color of a pallid, bronze hue as if it had become a mirror reflecting the ochre sand beneath it.

Every breath she took seemed somehow charged and she felt as if they had somehow descended to a lower elevation. But that was impossible. This was the desert, not the ocean floor. Yet, the pressure on her chest and her labored breathing continued.

By the time they made camp, both were drained and could barely manage to put their sleeping blankets on the hot sand before they each collapsed into a deep, all encompassing slumber.

When they arose the next day, the horizon all around them was painted a dark purple and the Taureg knew that something bad was heading their way.

"What is it?" Sinclair asked as she packed her sleeping gear in the heavy saddle bags tied behind her camel's hump. "I feel strange, as if my entire body is being charged with electricity."

"See that sky?' Bin Starkill pointed all around them. "There is a sandstorm coming our way and it has us completely surrounded. I've never seen anything like this."

"What do we do?"

"We ride like the devil is after us and hope to outrun it." He tapped his camel's leg and when it knelt, he jumped onto its back.

"But in which direction?" Sinclair inquired mounting her animal.

Bin Starkill shrugged, taking his reins in his hands. "What difference does it make? Give the beasts their heads and see where they go."

With that he cried out, pulled on the rains and kicked his camel to spur it on. The beast snorted, spiting out a wad of phlegm and started galloping. Sinclair repeated his actions and was soon charging alongside the desert born Bin Starkill. The third camel chased after them of its own volition as the Taureg couldn't be bothered pulling it along. Their chances of outracing the world-engulfing sandstorm were almost non-existent but they had to try.

With ground eating gaits, the Dromedaries raced across the desert, their riders huddled down behind their necks urging them to greater speeds.

All Sinclair could see was the ground flying by beneath her as she clung to her camel's long neck and prayed she wouldn't fall off. Around them the sky became darker as walls of grit and dust rose up to blot out the heavens.

This has got to be what the end of the world looks like, she thought.

As best she could estimate, they had been running straight out for almost a half hour when a new sound broke through her concentration as something different than the howling wind. The noise grew louder and lifting her head, she saw several Land Rovers and half-tracks emerge from the rising storm. The vehicles rushed ahead of them and then purposely slowed down until they had formed a barrier.

Her instincts were to try and go around them, but looking up, she saw Bin Starkill pulling on his reins and bringing his camel to a stop. Trusting his intentions, she did the same until both of them were standing still approximately thirty yards from the parked desert machines.

From each auto heavily armed Berbers materialized and stood facing them. From one of the half-tracks, a man in a tan suit with black riding boots, appeared followed by a tall, powerfully built fellow in military dress. Sinclair instantly recognized Arman El Shaira and his pet thug, Gunther Friedoff. She could see other people watching them from inside the other vehicles and knew somewhere among them was Mahmoud, the Guardian of the Tree.

"Who are you and why are you following us?" El Shaira called out to be heard over the escalating roar of the storm.

Nicola Sinclair, sat up straight and unwound the scarf over her face. "I'm surprised you don't know," she called out. "Your man there has been trying to kill me for the past few days."

El Shaira's kepi hat was torn from his head and he stumbled backward before turning to Friedoff. "You said they were dead!"

The big German gritted his teeth and clenched his hands into fists.

"You incompetent oaf!" El Shaira continued to berate his lieutenant.

Meanwhile Bin Starkill pulled his camel closer to Sinclair's so she could hear him. "When I say dismount, do it fast! If they don't kill us… the storm will."

Sand was whipping off the ground now and grit hit their faces.

"Don't just stand there!" El Shaira screamed at his men and pointed to Sinclair and Bin Starkill. "SHOOT THEM!"

The dozen Berbers raised their weapons and attempted to obey their master's order but none of their automatic weapons fired. Stunned, each man looked down at his weapon and kept trying to pull the trigger. But none of the Russian made AK-47s would work.

Then, before anyone fully realized what had happened, a massive surge of wind picked up two of the jeeps and hurled them skyward.

"NOW!" Bin Starkill shouted and jumped off his mount. Sinclair followed suit and he was there to catch her. They scrambled away as their camels bumped into each other in fear and then bolted away right into the wall of the black storm. Bin Starkill took hold of her hand and shouted again. "Cover your face as best you can and don't let go of my hand." He started running away from El Shaira and his troops.

A dark blue-black tidal wave of spinning wind slammed into the convoy. The half-tracks were knocked over and sent tumbling over the ground as if they were plastic toys. Several rolled over El Shaira's Berbers as they disappeared into the maelstrom. Other machines were ripped off the ground as were other men. The sandstorm roared like a living monster engulfing everything in its path.

Nicola Sinclair couldn't see anything, the world had become nothing but wind and sand and it cut into her exposed flesh. She only felt Bin Starkill pull her down to the ground and cover her body with his own. Trying to open her eyes, she saw that they were stretched out next to an outcrop of rock. It jutted out of the ground by a half foot, and realized her companion was taking advantage of what little protection it could afford them.

She hugged him fiercely and the air around them seemed to come alive and claw at them. The storm's noise rose in crescendo until she thought her head would explode. Then it was gone and the whirling dust devils dancing all around them became completely silent as if something had sucked out all the noise in the world.

Sinclair felt her body trembling just as the ground beneath her opened up and swallowed them both.

***

When Niki Sinclair opened her eyes again, she was stretched out on the floor of a tunnel. The earth beneath her was packed dirt and cool to the touch, while the walls rising up to either side of her were of a clay-like, porous rock and rose to a curved ceiling ten feet in height. *You could put an underground in here,* was her first thought. Then she remembered what had transpired just before she passed out.

She and Bin Starkill had sunk into the hot sands as if they were being consumed by the very desert itself. She vaguely recalled the sensation of falling and then nothing. She sat up with her back against the wall and touched her forehead lightly. Running her fingertips over her face, she could feel half a dozen tiny cuts, the results of the blistering sand that had horribly scoured their flesh in those last minutes of exposure. Her special Raybans were also missing; no doubt torn from her face by the savage winds.

She was still in her Bedouin robes and scarves…and she was alone.

Then she heard the screams. They were faint and seemed to originate far away down another branch of the tunnels. From her position she could see a juncture where four openings met. There was some kind of diffused lighting that made it possible for her see clearly. Just another mystery to add to all the others.

Climbing to her feet, she reached into her robes and pulled out her A.C.T.I.O.N. sword. Holding it out before her, she started down the corridor towards the direction the screams were coming from. As she neared the open conjuncture a Berber went running past her yelling at the top of his lungs. Two giant scorpions appeared from behind him, their multiple legs clacking across the tunnel floor. The fastest one seemed to leap upwards and one of its huge mandibles struck the fleeing Berber in the back knocking him to the ground. Then the scorpion, which had two tails and stingers, was atop the crying man and its stingers repeatedly cut into his body. The second monster joined the first in ravaging the now jerking remains of the fallen Berber.

The Katari! Sinclair remembered Mahmoud's descriptions of the creatures. Seeing them up close, the British agent realized just how much danger she was in. Each of the black bugs was three feet high and near six feet in length. With a hard exoskeleton and two poisonous stingers, they were the personification of a living, crawling nightmare.

Not waiting to see what would happen if they turned and saw her, Sinclair started jogging into another tunnel doing her best move quietly. She heard more screams seeming to come from all around her and with the ominous clacking sounds she now knew to be made by the hunting Katari.

Coming out of one tunnel, she ran into another juncture hub just as a Katari emerged from the opening across from hers. She stopped fast as did the monster. Then with its mandibles snapping outward, it rushed at her. Sinclair held her ground, clasping her blade with two hands and at the last possible second, twisted her body around like that of a Spanish matador. The Katari's claw swung past her and in a quick stroke, she swung down her sword and its unique blade sliced off the creature's sharp pincer. It made a screeching noise and twisted around, its two tails raised up high over its body pointing their barbs at her.

It attacked again and Sinclair dodged once more. One of the stingers came for her face and she chopped it off with a hard defensive stroke. Before the monstrosity could align itself for another strike, Sinclair stepped up to it and plunged her sword into its head, the specially treated steel cutting through it like a butcher's hatchet cleaving through a rack of bacon. The mutant scorpion shuddered and collapsed, a green ichor oozing from its mortal wound.

Panting, she pulled her sword free and started down another tunnel. The noises ahead of her were louder than before and amidst the voices screaming and the clacking of the Katari she heard the clashing of blades. Someone was putting up a good fight and she prayed they could hold out until she reached them.

Fifty yards into the tunnel and it curved around into another clearing; one filled with Berbers and other folks desperately battling almost a dozen Katari that had them surrounded. Some of the Berbers were using their rifles as clubs whereas they could not fire them.

"Well, don't just stand there!" a familiar voice in the middle of the melee called out to her. It was Bin Starkill and he was wielding two curved scimitars as he did his best to keep three Katari at bay. "I could use a little help here."

Sinclair clenched her teeth and charged into the fray, her sword raised above her head as she gave out with a passionate battle-cry. Like a possessed Viking berserker of old, the A.C.T.I.O.N. agent cut through the Katari from behind as most were focused on the dwindling human prey they had encircled. By the time they noticed her, she had brought down four of the monsters and both her sword and robes were covered with green syrupy goo.

Still, despite her best efforts, most of El Shaira's forces fell beneath the horrible scorpions until all that remained was Sinclair and Bin Starkill fighting back to back.

Without a word, the two of them continued hacking away at the Katari whose own numbers were also dwindling until, after almost fifteen minutes of non-stop battling, the last hard-shelled demon fell beneath their blades.

Sinclair stood frozen, afraid to let her guard down. All around them were the bodies of both men and monsters piled atop each other.

"It's over," Bin Starkill finally gasped. "For now, at least."

Sinclair felt her entire body shudder and together they stepped over the carcasses.

Bin Starkill sheathed one of his swords in the scabbard tied to his rope belt and used his free hand to support her as they began walking towards another corridor. This one looked empty and there seemed to be a stronger light at its far end. The weary duo moved along methodically putting one foot in front of the other, breathing slowly and keeping their swords ready.

As they neared the tunnel exit, a faltering figure entered and began to stumble towards them. The harsh light at his back cast the survivor as a black silhouette but the closer they got to each other, one gruesome element became clear; the man was missing his right arm.

"Professor Pareen!" Bin Starkill was able to recognize the old scientist with the gray beard by the time they were facing each other.

Hearing his name, the renowned archeologist looked at Bin Starkill and Sinclair and blinked several times. His face was a ghostly white as blood continued to flow from the empty socket. It coursed down his body and left a trail in the dirt behind him.

"I saw it," Pareen croaked. His eyes implored them. "It's real." Then he started to fall.

Bin Starkill dropped his sword and caught him so as to gently lower him to the ground. He cradled the old scholar's head in his arms. He looked up at Sinclair and said, "He's one of El Shaira's experts. He was in charge of the expedition."

"I saw it," Pareen repeated as his voice began to fade. He stared into Bin Starkill's gore smeared face and testified. "The Tree…it's real. Dear God, it's real." Then his eyes seemed to gloss over as his final breath escaped his lungs and his head fell back. Bin Starkill delicately closed Pareen's eyes and then carefully laid him down.

Picking up his sword, he rose up and looking from the dead man to Sinclair, pointed his sword to the glaring daylight before them. "It appears we've reached the end of our journey, Lady Action."

She grinned. "Then let's go and wrap this up, Ari. Whatever the end is, I'm glad to face it with you, Son of the Desert."

She extended her arm and he clasped it in his. "It has been my honor to fight by your side, dear lady. You are a warrior after my own heart."

Together, side by side they proceeded down the tunnel and a few minutes later they stepped out into a wide open arena. Both of them shaded their eyes from the glaring sun and the powder blue sky above them. Sinclair was instantly reminded of an ancient amphitheater, with the clearing before them surrounded by hills into which dozen of tunnels were dug. The arena was set in a depression and at its very center, rising over thirty feet into the air was a tree. It had a smooth white bark and its hundreds of branches were covered with vibrant green leaves, each possessing three to five lobes. The air was filled with a poignant fragrance the Taureg knew all too well.

"It's a fig tree," he told Sinclair. "The Tree of Life is a fig tree!"

Not being an expert on botany, Nicola Sinclair couldn't make any relevant comment to that fact. Although she was aware this type of deciduous tree was plentiful in this part of the world and considered one of the oldest trees in existence. Somehow that made sense.

But her attention to the tree was short as she saw the sand around it was littered the more remains of both people and Katari.

Then she saw something moving behind the massive bole of the tree. Out of its inky shadows Armin El Shaira stepped forth pushing Mahmoud before him. El Shaira held a scimitar pressed into his captive's back. The old blind storyteller was still holding on to his cane.

"Don't you ever tire of chasing after me?" El Shaira asked.

"It appears that's all come to an end," Sinclair stated the obvious.

"Oh, but this is only the beginning," El Shaira declared. "In a few minutes I am going to eat a few of these tasty figs and become immortal. And there is nothing you or your friend can do to stop me."

"I cannot permit that," Mahmoud said clearly, holding his cane up.

"Shut up, old man," El Shaira barked. "Your part in all this is finished. There's nothing you can do to stop me."

"Oh, foolish one, you have no power here." As Mahmoud spoke he began waving his cane around in the air. Immediately dozens of new Katari began emerging from the tunnels all around them.

Sinclair and Bin Starkill raised their swords ready for whatever happened next.

"Call them off!" El Shaira warned. "Or you will die here and now."

Old Mahmoud looked up at the sky with his blind orbs and smiled. "Why do you think I came back?" He tossed his cane away and instantly the Katari moved closer, their mandibles agitated…eager to rip into new flesh.

"Aghh..." A body suddenly flew out of the cave behind Sinclair and Bin Starkill and slammed into the tall Taureg. He and his attacker hit the ground and rolled over each other.

It was Gunther Friedoff, his face a mask of bleeding cuts. His surprise attack had knocked Bin Starkill's sword away and now the desert prince found himself being pummeled by the crazed German killer. His eyes wide with madness, spittle coming from his mouth, El Shaira's hired thug was raining down blow after blow on Bin Starkill.

Sinclair was about to come to his aid when El Shaira called out to her.

"You lose again!" He shoved his sword through Mahmoud's body, its tip ripping out from his chest. The old man cried out and then fell into the sand.

The Katari began to rush forward to exact their revenge. But Mahmoud wasn't dead and somehow managed to reach out, grab his cane and rolling to his hide, hold it up over his head. The gesture stopped the scorpions.

Seeing this, El Shaira laughed and turned to the Tree. He started to reach up for one of its low hanging branches with his free hand.

As he began to grab several of the purple fruit, Nicola Sinclair gave out another cry and charged. El Shaira turned around just as her sword came down aimed at his head. He parried with his own blade and pushed her back. She back-stepped two feet and skillfully diverted his own slashes. They began to circle each other under the overhanging branches, each becoming wary of the other's blade.

At the same time, Bin Starkill, who had kept his forearms up to ward off Friedoff's constant blows, finally managed to bring up his right knee and slam it into the German's back knocking him away. Then he rolled away to get clear and sprang to his feet. Both men faced each other, fists at ready.

"I'm going to kill you slowly, desert dog," Friedoff growled.

"Others have tried, Gunther Friedoff. I buried all of them."

Friedoff pivoted and snapped a side-kick at his foe. Bin Starkill blocked it with his hands and then grabbing the German's ankle, twisted it hard pulling him off his feet. Angrily, Friedoff jumped to his feet and threw a hard right that caught the Taureg in chest. Bin Starkill groaned and punched out with his own left nailing Friedoff in the nose. There was a crack of cartilage and the big man roared in pain. Bin Starkill followed up with a right that hit Friedoff on the side of the head and drove him back. He feebly tried to keep his hands up as the desert fighter weaved around him looking for another opening.

At the same time El Shaira grew frustrated as his repetitive lunges against the smaller woman were all deflected. For whatever strength he might possess, her fluid grace was proving to be the superior advantage. Desperate, he came at her whipping his scimitar in a figure 8 pattern, pushing her back even more. Then, before she knew what he was doing, El Shaira reached down with his empty hand, scooped up a handful of sand and tossed it into her face.

Nicola Sinclair, blinded, fell back defenseless.

Gunther Friedoff realized he was losing his contest with the tall, dusky Bin Starkill and made a final desperate assault. He opened his arms to try and tackle the Taureg, only to have Bin Starkill step out of his path and fall on him from behind. They fell to the ground and Starkill, having dropped onto Friedoff's back, quickly wrapped both his arms around his neck and clasped them together at the German's nape. Then, pushing down on the man's back, Bin Starkill pulled upward forcing his head backward….to the breaking point.

Friedoff scratched at the sand knowing he was doomed, his head stretched back until there was a loud cracking noise and his neck broke. He gave up a gurgling sound and his eyes rolled up in their sockets as his body went completely limp in death.

Unable to see clearly, Sinclair heard El Shaira cry out and purposely fell onto her back just as his blade whistled over her face. Then, before he could regain his balance, she sat up straight and sensing his body before, swung her sword around and felt it cut through his outer thigh. He screamed and retreated.

Wiping at her eyes with the back of her empty hand, Sinclair scrambled to her feet and as her vision returned, she saw her opponent limping at her, his scimitar coming around in a long arc aimed for her head. Instead of moving away, she stepped into him and swung her own sword at his onrushing stroke so that her edge met his wrist and cleanly cut off his hand.

As the hand and sword fell at their feet, El Shaira looked at her in shock, his eyes doubled their size. He was stunned.

Nicola Sinclair spun about fully and extending her sword arm, slashed with blinding speed so that it connected with El Shaira's neck. His head came off with a swish and dropped to the ground a second before his body did. Blood gushed from his neck soaking into the deep yellow sand.

***

Seeing Bin Starkill standing over the fallen Friedoff, Sinclair hurried over to Mahmoud and dropped to the ground beside him.

"It is finished?" he asked, still holding up his cane.

"Yes," she replied looking at the deep wound in his chest. "El Shaira is dead…without having eaten from the Tree."

Mahmoud smiled. "Your hand, give it to me."

She complied and he handed her his cane.

"Now command them to go, the Katari. They will not hurt you or the priest warrior."

"But you need help," she argued wanting to do something but knowing it was useless.

"It's all right, Sinclair," another voice said from behind her. "I'll take care of Mahmoud."

She looked up over her shoulder and there stood Alan Porter.

"Alan! You're alive!"

"Yes, I am. In fact I'm more alive than I've ever been before." His face seemed a bit more weathered with a beard just starting to come in but it was his eyes that she noticed. They were all white.

"Your eyes…you're blind."

"In one way," he smiled. "It's part of the job requirement, Sinclair."

"The job?"

"I'm now the Guardian. But please, do as Mahmoud said. The Katari are a skittish breed and it's best to shoo them away now."

Sinclair was still confused but having no better recourse, stood up while holding Mahmoud's cane over her head faced the deadly Katari. "Go away! I command you!"

The black armored creatures chattered wildly and then all of them turned and retreated back into the tunnels from which they had come. Within seconds all of them were gone.

Bin Starkill, sword in hand, walked over to stand beside Sinclair as Alan Porter bent down and picked up old Mahmoud in his arms.

"Are you ready, Mahmoud?"

The old Arab looked up at Porter. "Yes, my friend. It will be good to sleep at last."

"Farewell, good and faithful servant."

"Is he gone?" Sinclair asked.

Porter looked at her with his blind eyes. "From this world, yes, he is." Then he walked over to the base of the magnificent tree and there laid down Mahmoud's body. He stepped away to rejoin Sinclair and Bin Starkill. He held out his hand to Sinclair and she gave him the cane.

Alan Porter held up the cane to the Tree of Life and mouthed a silent prayer.

The tree began to vibrate, its limbs trembling.

Then the ground under Mahmoud's body opened and he slipped from view as its thick roots closed over him.

***

"So I gather you aren't coming back with us," Nicola Sinclair addressed her former A.C.T.I.O.N. colleague.

"Hardly," Porter concurred. "I wish I could explain it to you so you'd understand. For whatever reason, the Tree chose me to be its next Guardian. To do so, it had to give me true sight." He held a hand up to his blind eyes.

"What exactly does that mean?" Sinclair and Bin Starkill were sipping on water Porter had provided them immediately after they had seen to old Mahmoud's unique internment.

"It means I can see everything, Sinclair. The molecules in the sand, in your body…nothing his hidden from me. I see it all. How truly miraculous this world is, my dear. The Tree gave me all that."

"And for that, you must now be its protector."

"Yes. I just hope I'm as good at it as Mahmoud was."

Sinclair gave her friend a hug. "I wish you only the best, Alan."

"Thank you. So what are you going to tell them back A.C.T.I.O.N. ?"

"Right now, I don't know. They're going to think I went nuts with heatstroke."

"Ha, ha. Well, I'm sure you'll think of something. But now, I'm afraid its time for you and Ari to be on your way."

"And how exactly do we do that?" Bin Starkill wanted to know. "I've absolutely no idea where we are."

Alan Porter chuckled and pointed to the nearest tunnel before them. "There. Just follow that one. It will lead you away from here and to safety. Don't worry how, just trust me."

"Very well, what other choice do we have?" Bin Starkill patted Porter's arm. "It's been an honor to know you, my friend."

"Likewise, Ari. Now go on and get Nicola home."

Impulsively Niki gave Porter a kiss on the cheek. "Good-bye, Alan."

"Till we meet again, Lady Action."

Sinclair and Bin Starkill started down the tunnel without looking back.

***

They had been walking for an hour, both recognizing that unlike the earlier tunnels, this one had no separate adjoining branches and simply went in one direction. When they saw the bright light ahead they knew they had reached the end. The tunnel came to a steep slope and with some effort they managed to climb it and come out into the open once again.

No sooner had they done so than the ground beneath them rumbled and they moved away just as the opening they had exited from was completely filled with sand and all traces of it gone in an instant.

"Well, I guess we won't be going back that way?' Bin Starkill commented wryly.

Nicola Sinclair was going to agree when a braying cry made them both whirled around.

Standing twenty yards in front of them, munching on a clump of desert brush were their three camels. All of them looked at Sinclair and Bin Starkill as if they didn't have a care in the world, their mouths chewing happily on the juicy leaves.

"I don't believe it!" Bin Starkill shook his head. He examined the back of the load-camel and discovered most of their supplies were still tied to the saddle-packs.

"It's all here," he said somewhat dumfounded.

"Are you really surprised?" Sinclair asked. "After everything we've been through?"

"Ha, you have a point, Lady Action. Come, let us get on these wonderful animals and let them take us home."

Five minutes later, riding side by side, Lady Action and Gordon Ari Bin Starkill began their trek out of the Deep Desert.

As they started off, Bin Starkill recited an old Taureg poem.

"The desert is my cradle, I was born here
The desert is my road, I travel here
The desert is my grave, I will die here."

***

CAIRO
One Month Later

Jacques Marceau was ushered into the Falal El Shaira's private office. She sat behind her desk looking at him coolly. Dressed in the latest French fashions, she was a cruel beauty.

She was also a vengeful one.

"Monsieur Marceau, it is good to see you again."

"Ahem...*oui, Madame*. Though I am sorry it has to be under such tragic circumstances."

"Spare me your sympathies, sir. Considering the time that has elapsed since my brother launched his expedition, I've reconciled myself to the fact that he has failed and is most likely dead."

"I am so sorry, Madame."

Falal pushed away from her desk and stood. "You brought the pictures... the ones of the British agent involved."

"Oui, Madame. I have them right here." Marceau reached into his attaché case, found the three photographs and stepping closer, handed them to the new C.E.O. of El Shaira Unlimited.

She studied the woman in the pictures. "And you say her name is Sinclair."

"Yes, Nicola Sinclair....of A.C.T.I.O.N."

Falal nodded. She spoke to the photo. "Wherever you are, Nicola Sinclair, one day I will find you and on that day you will wish you had never been born."

THE END

ABOUT OUR CREATORS

AUTHOR -

RON FORTIER – Comics and pulps writer/editor best known for his work on the Green Hornet comic series and Terminator – Burning Earth with Alex Ross. He won the Pulp Factory Award for Best Pulp Short Story of 2011 for "Vengeance Is Mine," which appeared in Moonstone's The Avenger – Justice Inc. and in 2012 for "The Ghoul," from the anthology Monster Aces. He is the Managing Editor of Airship 27 Productions, a New Pulp Fiction publisher and writes the continuing adventures of both his own character, Brother Bones – the Undead Avenger and the classic pulp hero, Captain Hazzard – Champion of Justice.

COVER ARTIST –

TED HAMMOND - is a Canadian artist who has been creating amazing art for over twenty years. His work has appeared in magazines, ads, books and graphic novels just to name a few. Go to (www.tedhammond.com) to contact him and check out more of his work!

CAPTAIN ACTION
Pulp Hero
CAPTAIN ACTION
RIDDLE of the GLOWING MEN
JIM BEARD
One of the most popular heroes of the 1960s returns in his first ever full-length novel. Super-spy and master of disguise, Miles Drake, aka Captain Action investigates the "Riddle of the Glowing Men," by writer Jim Beard. Foreign assassins are sent to kill Captain Action and though he manages to defeat them, it is their lifeless bodies that pose the greater mystery as they give off a green, glowing radiation.
Teamed with a beautiful and seductive Russian Agent, Captain Action travels to the barren, frozen wastelands of Siberia where the secret behind the glowing men lies buried in a fantastic, lost underground world. It is a secret also pur- sued by his most dangerous nemesis, the insidious Dr. Evil. What is this strange power hidden beneath the earth that could destroy all of mankind and who will unlock its mysteries first?
"Riddle of the Glowing Men," is a classic pulp thriller packed with enough intrigue, daring escapes and breakneck adventure to fill a dozen books. Featuring a stunning cover by artist Nick Runge and interior illustrations by award winning artist, Rob Davis, it presents a well loved hero to a new audience eager to experience his special brand of two-fisted battling, Captain Action style!
AN AIRSHIP 27 PRODUCTION
AIRSHIP27HANGAR.COM
New PULP
PULP FICTION FOR A NEW GENERATION!
AVAILABLE AT AMAZON.COM AND AS AN EBOOK PDF AT AIRSHIP27HANGAR.COM
™ & © Captain Action Enterprises, LLC www.CaptainAction.com

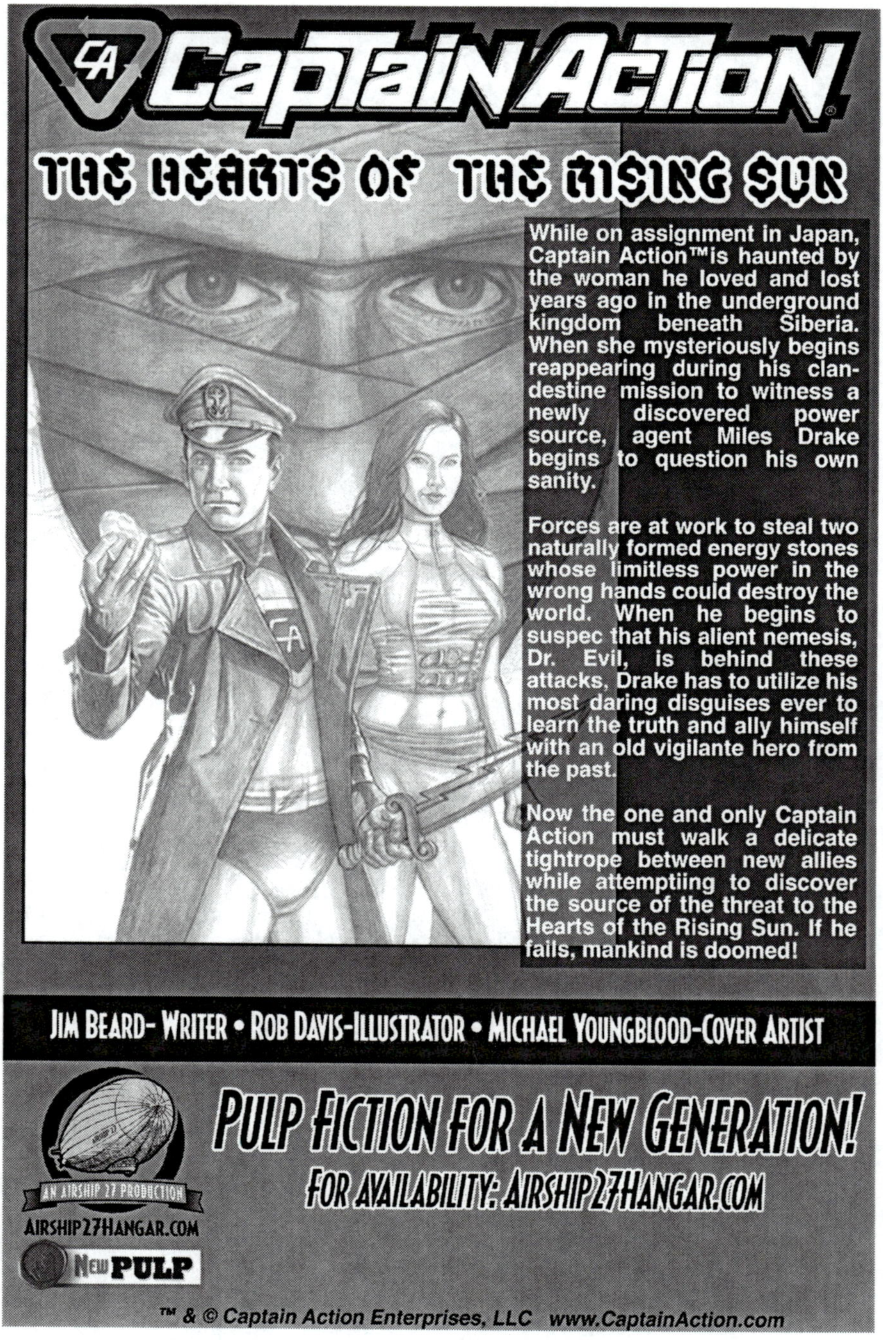
CA
Captain Action®
THE HEARTS OF THE RISING SUN
While on assignment in Japan, Captain Action™is haunted by the woman he loved and lost years ago in the underground kingdom beneath Siberia. When she mysteriously begins reappearing during his clandestine mission to witness a newly discovered power source, agent Miles Drake begins to question his own sanity.
Forces are at work to steal two naturally formed energy stones whose limitless power in the wrong hands could destroy the world. When he begins to suspec that his alient nemesis, Dr. Evil, is behind these attacks, Drake has to utilize his most daring disguises ever to learn the truth and ally himself with an old vigilante hero from the past.
Now the one and only Captain Action must walk a delicate tightrope between new allies while attemptiing to discover the source of the threat to the Hearts of the Rising Sun. If he fails, mankind is doomed!
JIM BEARD- WRITER • ROB DAVIS-ILLUSTRATOR • MICHAEL YOUNGBLOOD-COVER ARTIST
AN AIRSHIP 27 PRODUCTION
AIRSHIP27HANGAR.COM
NEW PULP
PULP FICTION FOR A NEW GENERATION!
FOR AVAILABILITY: AIRSHIP27HANGAR.COM
™ & © Captain Action Enterprises, LLC www.CaptainAction.com

Coming Soon!
SECRET AGENT "X"
THE MAN OF A THOUSAND FACES
Agent X in Action!
Volume Five!
The greatest pulp spy of them all returns in this, the action packed fifth volume of brand new Secret Agent X adventures by today's top New Pulp writers.
Within these pages the Man of a Thousand Faces squares off against a deadly foreign spy in a climatic battle amongst the clouds; faces terror on the high seas as he duels a modern day Captain Nemo and then battles with a beautiful, cunning criminal mastermind. Here are thrills upon thrills in four brand new tales by J. Walt Layne, Andy Fix, Fred Adams Jr. and Frank Schildiner.
Secret Agent X is one of the most popular heroes ever to emerge from the classic pulps. Now's he back; a one man army defending the country he loves against all who would threaten her. This is pulp fiction at its best!
AN AIRSHIP 27 PRODUCTION
AIRSHIP27HANGAR.COM
NEW PULP
PULP FICTION FOR A NEW GENERATION!
FOR AVAILABILITY GO TO AIRSHIP27HANGAR.COM

CPSIA information can be obtained
at www.ICGtesting.com
Printed in the USA
FSOW02n0402080216
16683FS

9 780692 459454